Super
SCARY
STORIES
for Sleep-Overs

By Q. L. Pearce
Illustrated by Dwight Been

An RGA Book

PRICE STERN SLOAN
Los Angeles

To the seventh grade students of
Vineyard Junior High School, 1994–95.
—Q. L. P.

To my nieces and nephews.
—D. M. B.

Copyright © 1995 by RGA Publishing Group, Inc.
Published by Price Stern Sloan, Inc.,
A member of the Putnam & Grosset Group, New York, New York.

ISBN: 0-8431-3915-3
First Edition
1 3 5 7 9 10 8 6 4 2

Library of Congress Cataloging-in-Publication Data

Pearce, Q. L. (Querida Lee)
    Super scary stories for sleep-overs / by Q. L. Pearce : illustrated by Dwight Been.
        p.   cm.
    "An RGA book."
    Summary: A collection of spooky short stories, including "It waits," "The family honor," "Flesh and blood," and "Horror in the center ring."
    ISBN 0-8431-3915-3
    1. Horror tales, American. 2. Children's stories, American.
[1. Horror stories. 2. Short stories.] I. Been, Dwight, ill.
II. Title.
PZ7.P31495Su 1995
[Fic]—dc20   95–1986
                                                      CIP
                                                      AC

Designed by Michele Lanci-Altomare

Contents

Flesh and Blood

harlie let out a huff when he saw the dark rainclouds.

"Not today," he whined. "The guys and I were going to play soccer." He was standing outside with his father who was just getting into his car to go to work.

His father slammed the car door, and rolled down the window. "You'll just have to find something to do indoors." He paused for a second. "I've got it. There's a new exhibit from Egypt at the museum. Why don't you check it out?"

"Thanks, Dad," Charlie said unenthusiastically.

His father shrugged. "Well, I tried," he said, rolling up the window and starting the car.

Charlie watched his father drive off, then went inside and flopped down on a well-worn easy chair. The newspaper was on the coffee table, and Charlie absentmindedly began to flip through it when an article about the Egyptian exhibit caught his eye.

A moment later he was on the phone with his friend Sean.

"It sounds really cool!" Charlie said excitedly. "It's a real mummy on loan to the Single Falls History Museum. And get this—the article says that the mummy was some royal person who got into big trouble and was cursed!"

Sean snickered. "Yeah right." Then he let out a big sigh. "Well, there's nothing better to do."

Within an hour Charlie and Sean were waiting in the lobby of the museum. Sean had also called Gordon and Kristy to join them, and the two were walking up already.

"Hey, guys," said Gordon, a lanky boy wearing jeans and a sweat shirt.

"Hey, Gordon," Sean responded. "Hey, Kristy," he called to a young girl pushing her way through the turnstile.

Kristy grinned. "So let's go see this creepy mummy dude," she said. "Maybe he's cute."

The museum was made up of five small, separate wings. The Egyptology wing had scale models of the pyramids and displays of ancient Egyptian relics. In the middle of the room was the mummy, and the kids made a beeline for it.

"Wow, cool!" Gordon exclaimed, leaning over the railing. The sarcophagus was tilted up, making it easier for the kids to see the dry, shriveled body inside.

"Gross," said Kristy, turning away. The mummy was the dark color of swamp mud. Bits of rotted cloth hung from it, and a few wiry tufts of hair seemed plastered to the grinning skull.

"Yep," Charlie said with a smile. "There he is . . . in the flesh, so to speak."

Kristy giggled at Charlie's joke, then went over to read the sign on the wall beside the display. "It says here that he was an Egyptian prince," she reported. "It seems he was a nasty character and a lot of people disappeared during his reign. "Yuck!" she shrieked in disgust. "He was accused of draining blood from others. It says he thought the life force of his victims would keep him young so he could live forever. When he got caught, they killed him by draining away all of *his* blood."

"Freaky." Sean gazed in awe at the dry corpse. "So much for living forever. He's dead as a doornail."

Gordon widened his eyes. "Maybe not. Perhaps," he kidded in a deep, heavily accented voice, "perhaps he is merely sleeeeeeping. And when the moon is full he will awake and take his revenge." The others chuckled as Gordon drew one arm into his chest, held the other arm out, and limped, stiff-legged, toward Kristy.

"Go away, you idiot!" She laughed and pushed him away.

Charlie stared at the mummy. "Maybe Gordon's onto something," he mused.

Kristy shook her head. "Uh-uh. They dug up this guy nearly a year ago and he hasn't moved a muscle . . . full moon or not."

"Maybe conditions weren't right," Gordon said half seriously. "Or maybe he really *does* get out of his coffin and stalk the city at night. No one can watch him every minute, so there's no way to know for sure."

7

"Yes there is!" Charlie said enthusiastically. We could stay over tonight and watch him! Looks like the old guy could use some company anyhow."

Gordon shook his head. "Naw, my mom expects me home by supper time. Besides, the guards won't let us stay in here all night."

"You can call your mom and say you're spending the night at my house. We can all come up with something," Charlie reasoned. "And those old guards won't be any problem. We can hide in the bathroom until they lock up. The museum doesn't even have a night watchman, just a guard service that drives by every once in a while. I know because my uncle Arlo works for the service."

Kristy didn't seem convinced. "I don't know," she said hesitantly. "What if we want to get out?"

Charlie grinned. "There's a window by the delivery entrance. Arlo's complained that he's found it open a couple of times. I'll just check to make sure it isn't latched."

"But the alarm system will go off if we go through the window," Gordon pointed out.

"So what?" Sean said, grinning. "We'll be long gone by then. I say we do it."

"C'mon," Charlie coaxed. "It'll be fun!"

Gordon and Kristy looked at each other and nodded. Then they each went off to call home.

• • • • • • • • • • •

The guard opened the bathroom door and stepped inside for

a final check before closing for the night. Standing up on the toilet in the last stall, Charlie held his breath. Finally the guard let the door swing shut and Charlie let out a big sigh. Sean and Gordon, in stalls on either side of him, did the same. They waited a few more moments, then Sean tiptoed to the door and peered out.

"He's gone," Sean whispered hoarsely. Then all of a sudden he drew back. "Somebody's coming!"

The boys pressed themselves against the wall as the door swung slowly open again.

"Having fun?" Kristy asked, peeking around at them. "You guys look pale," she said, laughing.

"Very funny," Charlie muttered. "Look, it's getting dark. Maybe we could find some of the guards' flashlights. I don't feel like sitting around in here if we can't see anything."

"I've got a penlight on my key chain," Gordon offered. "We can use it to go through the storage closets."

After a search through a couple of closets, Gordon's idea paid off, and the four kids now shared two flashlights.

"It sure looks different in here now," Gordon murmured as they made their way to the Egyptology wing. "It's spooky."

A dim light glowed here and there from various wall displays. It was definitely spooky, especially with each one of their footsteps echoing on the ceramic tile floor.

"Maybe this wasn't such a good idea," Sean muttered.

Suddenly Kristy froze. "What was that?" she cried out.

Sean turned his flashlight in the direction of a rustling sound. The beam fell on a huge, shimmering face with blood-red eyes and sharply pointed teeth.

"YYYYYEEEEEAAAAAA!!" Gordon yelled.

"Chill out!" Charlie shot back. "It's only a mask on the wall." He passed his light around the edge of the image so everyone could see the long, moss-green feathers that decorated it. One feather was moving slightly, creating the rustling sound. "There must be some air coming in from a vent," he guessed, trying to slow his rapidly beating heart.

"Well, I've had enough," Gordon said firmly. "You can call me a chicken if you want, but I'm leaving."

"I'm with Gordie," Kristy agreed. "You guys can stay, but I'm going home. Where's that window, Charlie?"

Sean looked at Charlie. "They're right," he said. "There's no point in doing this if it isn't any fun. Let's go."

Charlie finally agreed, then led them through the spooky Egyptology wing, down a series of halls, and out the back to the delivery entrance. "There it is," Charlie said, shining his light toward a small window about six feet up the wall. "See, the latch isn't hooked." He pointed to a big crate. "Help me push that underneath so we can reach it."

Quickly the four kids shoved the crate over.

"OW!" Sean complained. He held up a cut thumb for the others to see. "I'm going to the bathroom to wash it off. Gordie, hand me that flashlight. And don't you guys leave without me, OK? I'll be right back."

"Ah, fresh blood," Gordon said jokingly. "If there are any night creatures around, that bloody thumb should get their attention. Maybe it'll even wake up old King Tut in there."

"Shut up!" Kristy demanded. She was almost in tears.

"Well, excuuuuse me! I was just joking. Don't have a cow. We'll be out of here in a minute."

"Maybe we won't," Charlie said softly. "There are bars

across the window that are bolted from the outside. That must have been Uncle Arlo's idea."

"So now what are we going to do?" Kristy moaned.

"We could just stay here until the morning, then tell them we got locked in by accident," Charlie suggested.

Kristy shook her head. "I don't want to stay here all night. This place gives me the creeps."

Charlie jumped off the crate, snagging the sleeve of his dark blue sweater. "Then we'll have to call somebody to come get us," he said finally. "We can use a pay phone."

"Boy, are we going to be in trouble when—" Gordon began.

"Wait!" Charlie held up his hand. "I heard something. Hey . . . where's Sean?"

Kristy pointed a trembling finger toward the door that led back into the main part of the museum. "I—I thought he said he was going to the bathroom, right?" she stammered.

"Well, he's been gone a long time," Charlie said. "We have to look for him." He picked up his flashlight and motioned for the others to follow. "Sean?" he called timidly.

Silence.

"Sean, this isn't funny," he called again as they entered the room where the mummy was. Just then, Charlie's foot kicked something, and he bent down to pick it up.

"The other flashlight," Kristy said softly. "The one Sean took with him."

Suddenly Gordon gasped and grabbed Charlie's wrist, turning it so the flashlight beam fell on something just below the sarcophagus. It was Sean, lying on the floor in a crumpled heap.

"Oh, no!" Kristy raced to the boy and turned him over, then covered her mouth to hold back a scream. Sean was

11

pale. His lips looked pasty white and his skin was slightly shriveled.

"I don't believe this," Gordon said with a gasp, barely able to speak. "The mummy . . . look at the mummy." He leaned in to get a better look as if he couldn't believe his eyes.

Charlie felt as if something had sucked the air completely from his chest when he saw that the mummy's flesh looked fresher and more lifelike. The fingers looked as if they could simply reach out and . . .

"Look out!" he screamed. But it was too late. The mummy had gripped Gordon around the neck and lifted him off his feet as if the 110-pound boy weighed nothing.

"Help me!" Gordon shrieked, trying to pry away the mummy's fingers, now squeezing his throat. Lunging forward, Charlie grabbed Gordon's shoulders and tried to pull him away, while Kristy picked up a carved stone figure from a nearby display and beat at the mummy's powerful arms. But nothing seemed to stop the wretched thing, and within seconds Gordon went limp. Charlie and Kristy backed away as they saw their friend's skin slowly dry and shrivel, while that of the mummy appeared even more vital.

Then the life-sucking creature tossed Gordon's body aside, and clumsily began to struggle from the sarcophagus.

"We've got to get out of here!" Charlie yelled, grabbing Kristy by the hand.

"How?" she screamed. "We can't get by it!"

The grotesque being drew in a raspy, labored breath that sounded like the wind rushing down the corridors of an ancient tomb. It threw back its head and howled, raising its

nearly rejuvenated arms into the air. Then it stopped as if to listen. Slowly it turned from one side to another.

"Can it see us?" Kristy whispered.

In answer, the thing turned toward them and moved awkwardly in their direction.

"Let's rush it, then split off to either side of it," Charlie whispered. And with no other choice, the two terrified kids raced toward the mummy, then skirted around it. They dashed for the bank of telephones in the lobby, then stood there helplessly. Neither had any change.

Charlie turned his pockets inside out and only came up with dollar bills.

"What are we going to do?" Kristy cried.

"Listen!" Charlie put his hand over her mouth. The creature's labored breathing echoed in the main chamber. "We've got to hide." Looking frantically around, the two finally decided on a small side room with a display of Civil War furniture. Together they slid under a huge canopied bed just as the sound of heavy footsteps stopped right outside the entrance to the room. Charlie squeezed Kristy's hand. He could feel that she was shaking uncontrollably. He was in pretty bad shape, too. Droplets of sweat stung his eyes, but he was afraid to brush them away.

Everything was very still—*too* still. Suddenly Kristy screeched and began to slide from under the bed, feet first. "It's got my foot!" she cried, clawing at the floor.

Charlie grabbed onto her hands, but he could feel her slipping away from him. Then all at once, Kristy was wrenched out of his grasp.

Covering his ears to block out the sound of her tortured struggle, Charlie knew there was nothing he could do. Then he felt a powerful hand brush his own foot. *It's looking for me!* his mind shrieked. He kicked at the mummy's fingers and rolled out from the other side of the bed. In the dim light from a wall display he could see that the mummy's body was almost completely renewed. All it needed was the life force of *one* more victim. But Charlie was determined to defy the monster. Dashing toward the main hall, he could see that the windows were barred there, too.

Charlie knew the front door was his only chance. He *had* to go for it, or the mummy would find him sooner or later.

Making up his mind, he picked up a chair and tossed it into a tall glass display that housed Early American farm tools. The glass shattered, showering the room with sharp splinters that bit through Charlie's sneakers. He inched toward the display and grabbed a long metal bar once used as a hoe. Then, racing to the front door, he began to pry at the lock, and to his relief a high-pitched alarm began to scream into the night.

"Please open!" Charlie cried.

Without turning, he could sense that the thing was behind him, perhaps only inches away. He could smell the stench of something that had ceased living many centuries ago . . . something that shouldn't be walking the earth again, but was. He felt the lock snap and suddenly give way. The door flew open and a rush of cold air burst in.

• • • • • • • • • •

The first police car flew into the parking lot and screeched to a halt in a flurry of flying gravel.

"Look!" one of the officers yelled. "There's someone running toward the back of the building!"

"I'll get him," the second officer responded as she threw open her door and charged after the retreating figure.

Moments later she returned. "I lost him," she said, glancing at the three other cars that had arrived. "What's going on, Sergeant?"

"It's a lot more than just a break-in," her partner answered. He pointed to a body just inside the front door.

The female officer gasped and turned away. There, wearing a dark blue sweater, were the remains of a body—it was totally dry and withered.

"There're three more inside," another officer said, stepping out through the door. "This is impossible! What could have happened here?"

The female officer glanced up. "There's at least one person out there who knows," she said solemnly. "And we're going to have to try to find him."

From among the shadows on a hilltop overlooking the museum, something drew a deep, cool breath of air into fresh lungs. It felt the warm blood flowing once again through its body. And with its newly formed eyes, it gazed down at the lights of the small town that housed its unsuspecting prey . . . and it smiled.

The Room at the End of the Hall

renda's mom shook her head and pointing out of the car window. "Will you look at that?"

Brenda saw that her mom was indicating the weather-worn mailbox at the edge of the overgrown front yard, which was leaning at a crazy angle.

Her dad pulled the family car into the dirt driveway and slowed to a stop. "Movers must have run into it," he speculated as he opened his car door, stepped out, and walked over for a better look. Grabbing the slightly dented post with both hands, he pulled the mailbox back into its proper position, then headed back to the car.

"Check it out, Dad," Brenda's eight-year-old brother, Ted, snickered as the post slowly keeled over again.

Her father looked back, shrugged, then slid back into the driver's seat. "I'll take care of it later," he said as he started the engine. "We have plenty to do already if we're going to transform this place into our home."

Brenda turned her attention to the old house at the end of the driveway. Even though the summer morning was clear and sunny, the two-story house looked dreary, as if a cloud hung over it. Something about the place definitely made her feel uneasy. The once white walls had grayed with age, and a few shingles were missing from the roof, but that wasn't all. No, the old house had an eerie feeling about it, so much so that Brenda actually shivered slightly as her dad pulled the car up alongside the wide wooden porch.

"It may not look too great yet, but we'll whip it into shape," her mom said brightly, helping Brenda's four-year-old sister, Tina, out of her seat belt. "They just don't have houses like this in California—not ones we can afford, anyway." She smiled. "You kids are going to be surprised at how big it is inside."

"Don't mention California," Ted said with a pout. "I still don't understand why Dad can't be a doctor *there.*"

Brenda watched her mother stiffen slightly as a frown tugged at the corners of her mouth. "We live in Iowa now, Ted," she said firmly, as she adjusted Tina's pigtails. "You'll have to make the best of it."

Their dad pulled open the screen door, fumbled with his keys for a moment, then unlocked the front door. "*Voila,*" he said, pushing it open with a flourish. "Our new home."

Brenda's footsteps echoed on the hardwood floor as she stepped inside. She was surprised at the size of the entryway that led into the huge main room. "Wow, this is great!" she said sincerely. "Are the bedrooms upstairs?" Then she glanced sideways at her brother. "I get first pick since I'm the oldest."

Ted started to protest, but their dad cut him off.

"That sounds fair to me," he said.

"Cool!" Brenda exclaimed as she worked her way around the stacks of cardboard boxes to a wide staircase that rose along the wall to the right of the front door. "I'm going to pick out my room right now!"

Gripping the smooth, curved banister, Brenda counted the stairs one by one as she went up. At the twenty-second step she found herself in a long hallway with several doors on either side all opened . . . except for the one at the end.

Making her way down the hall, she stopped and stared at the closed door. Suddenly a weird feeling passed over her, and for just a moment she felt drawn to the room. She swayed slightly as if she might lose her balance.

"Whoa," she said aloud, thinking that maybe she had run up the stairs a little too quickly.

The uncomfortable feeling passed. Brenda turned and went back down the hall to inspect each room . . . until she found herself back at the closed door. An unsettling notion flickered through her mind. *I know this room*, she thought, *I've been here before*.

"That's crazy," she mumbled under her breath, then reached for the knob and turned it. "I've never been to Iowa before."

The door opened with a light click and swung silently inward. Brenda carefully studied the room. Larger than any of the others except the one her mom and dad had chosen, it

was painted a pale blue, and it had two large, wood-framed windows that looked down onto the backyard.

"*All right*, this looks cool," Brenda said and moved to step inside. But all at once the muscles in her stomach inexplicably tightened, and she felt a freakish surge of heat flood through her body. As a bolt of terror raced up her spine, she stumbled backward . . . right into a pair of hands that broke her fall.

"TED!" she yelled half in fear and half in relief.

"Who'd you expect? I live here now, too, remember?" he said sarcastically. "Now get off my foot. You're not exactly weightless, you know."

Brenda moved her foot and scowled at her brother. "Look," she shot back. "It's not my fault we had to move. So don't take it out on *me*."

"Of course not," he said with a smirk. "I wouldn't do anything to upset the family favorite. I suppose you've already picked out the biggest bedroom for yourself, right?"

Brenda glanced into the blue room. Something about it gave her the creeps, and she didn't want to even step across the threshold. "No. I want the room right at the top of the stairs. You can have this one if you want. It's the biggest besides Mom and Dad's."

Ted narrowed his eyes suspiciously. "What's wrong with it?"

"Nothing," Brenda lied. "I just like the other one better." She tried to cover up her nervousness by changing the subject. "Come on, let's go check out the backyard."

• • • • • • • • • • •

By the time she got ready for bed that night, Brenda was exhausted. For hours the entire family had moved furniture around and distributed boxes to the proper rooms. Even Tina had dragged a small box of toys clumsily up the stairs . . . *thump . . . thump . . . thump.*

Too busy to think of much else but where to put everything, Brenda hadn't thought about the room at the end of the hall the entire day. But now in the quiet of her new room, she recalled the creepy feeling she'd had that somehow it had been familiar to her. In fact, just thinking about it made her stomach feel a little queasy, and she tried to calm herself by listening to the sounds of the crickets outside in the tall, dry grass.

Then she heard another sound. It was very soft, so Brenda had to strain her ears to figure out what it was. Finally she realized that someone was crying, and it was coming from the room at the end of the hall.

"Ted?" Brenda sat up and listened again. Yes, the crying was definitely coming from her brother's room. Shaking her head, she climbed out of bed. "He really is being a baby about this move," she whispered to herself.

After tiptoeing down the hall, she stood in front of Ted's closed door and carefully put her ear up against it.

The sound was much fainter now, as if it were coming from somewhere else. She was about to call out to Ted to see if she could make him feel any better—she *was* his older sister, after all, and it was kind of her duty—when she remembered his "weightless" crack earlier in the day.

He'll be OK by tomorrow, she thought, yawning, as she walked back to her room. Stretching out on her bed, she made a promise to herself to try to be nicer to Ted until he felt better about the move. Then just before she drifted off to sleep, she noticed the crying had stopped.

• • • • • • • • • • •

"Morning, honey," her mom said, smiling, as Brenda entered the kitchen the next morning. "There's fresh-squeezed orange juice in the refrigerator. Would you mind pouring some for everyone and putting it on the table?"

"No problem," Brenda answered, as she took five glasses from the cupboard and started to put one at each place. Then she stopped.

"Mom, who isn't eating breakfast with us?" she asked.

"What do you mean, dear?" her mom responded while buttering toast.

"There're only four places," Brenda pointed out.

Her father walked into the kitchen carrying a giggling Tina.

"Of course there're only four places," he said with a smile. "Why? Were you expecting company?"

Brenda frowned. "What about Ted?"

"Ted who?" her dad said as he situated Tina in her chair and then sat down himself.

Brenda looked at both of her parents, then started to laugh. "OK, what's the joke? I'll admit that sometimes I wish we could send Ted to the moon, but we're stuck with him."

Brenda's mom and dad gave each other a quizzical look.

"C'mon, you guys." Brenda felt her smile fade. "This isn't funny anymore. I'm talking about Ted . . . my brother?

You know . . . your son? The weird kid in the room at the end of the hall?"

Her mom shook her head. "Brenda," she said slowly. "You're right. This isn't funny. We don't have a son named Ted. We don't have a son at all. And the room at the end of the hall is Tina's. It has been for months, ever since we moved here."

For a moment everyone sat in complete silence. Brenda tried to make some sort of sense out of what her parents were saying.

Finally Tina broke the stillness. "I know a boy named Ted at school," she offered in a childish whisper. "He pushed me off the swings last week."

Speechless and about to break into tears, Brenda jumped up from the table and raced from the kitchen. As she ran to the stairs she could see that there were no longer any boxes in the living room. Everything was neatly in its place as if it had been that way for some time.

At the top of the stairs she stopped. Her head was spinning. She lurched to the end of the hall and opened the door to the room. Inside she saw Tina's small bed with a sky blue comforter on it. At the windows were ruffly blue curtains, and a shelf unit on the opposite wall was lined with dolls and stuffed animals. Her parents were right; this was definitely Tina's room.

"But how can this be?" she whispered, noticing that there was something else, too: a faint smell of charred wood and ash.

"You see?" Brenda's dad said softly as he walked up behind her and placed his hands gently on her shoulders.

Brenda didn't even try to wipe away the tears that were running down her cheeks. "This is crazy," she moaned. "I don't understand what's happening."

Her father smiled and gently turned her face toward his. "It isn't crazy, honey," he said. "You're obviously upset about something." He paused, then wiped a tear from her eye. "I tell you what. Maybe you're just tired. You've been working very hard at school. Why not just take the day off and stay in bed? Once you're rested up everything will be fine." He gave her a warm hug. "Listen, I've got plenty of work that I can do here, so you won't be alone. My partner can see my patients today, OK? So should I go call my office?"

Brenda didn't answer, and she didn't resist as her father guided her back to her room. She suddenly felt extremely tired. *It's just a dream*, she thought as he tucked her into bed. *I'll wake up soon and everything will be back to normal.*

It was early afternoon when Brenda awoke. She slipped out of bed and tiptoed to the top of the stairs. She could hear her father's voice. He was in the den downstairs talking on the phone to someone at his office.

Turning, she moved cautiously to the room at the end of the hall and peeked inside. Everything was as it had been that morning. Next she slipped into her parents' room. Against one wall stood a large oak chest of drawers. On the chest was a handmade lace runner, three cut-crystal perfume bottles, a small wooden bowl where her dad kept the change he emptied from his pockets, and a collection of family photographs in pretty frames. She looked at one photo after another and saw the smiling faces of her mom, dad, Tina, and herself. But there were no photos of Ted.

Returning to her own room, she dressed quickly and hurried downstairs. When she opened the kitchen door it was remarkably cold outside for summer, but then she remembered that if several months had really gone by it could be fall or even winter. She grabbed her jacket from a hook by the door and slipped out.

Running to the garage, Brenda looked inside. Well, at least her dad's car was there, along with her bicycle and Tina's old tricycle. Surely Ted's bike would be there too . . . or his skateboard . . . or something to prove that he had ever existed. But there was nothing.

"What is happening?" she groaned. "Have I lost my mind?"

• • • • • • • • • • •

That night at dinner, Brenda told her mom and dad that she felt much better, then chose to be silent. It wouldn't help to have them thinking that she was nuts, so keeping quiet until she figured things out seemed like the answer.

Tina chattered about her busy day at preschool, and her mom talked about the new project she was planning at the university. Every once in a while Brenda noticed her parents glance at her and then look worriedly at each other. Trying to appear as normal as possible, Brenda helped with the dishes after supper. Then claiming to still be tired, she asked to be excused.

As she trudged up the stairs, Brenda noticed that she actually was exhausted. In fact, she had a little trouble breathing, and what she did take into her lungs had the scent of something burnt. She looked around for signs of smoke, but there were none.

Trying to shrug everything off as just her imagination, she climbed wearily into bed. But there was no way she could fall asleep. Instead, Brenda lay awake for a long time, listening as her parents put Tina to bed in the blue room at the end of the hall—Ted's old room. She heard the television go on for a while, and soon all was quiet. After a few more minutes of staring into the darkness, Brenda finally drifted off into a light, troubled sleep.

But just a few hours later, after a lot of tossing and turning, Brenda opened her eyes. Once again she heard someone crying softly down the hall. She looked at the glowing numbers on her digital clock. It was 12:03.

"Tina?" she whispered, sitting up as she heard the cries growing slightly louder.

It sounded as if her little sister was sobbing . . . just like Ted once did. A shudder ran through her and she leaped out of bed.

Quickly running down the hall, she threw open what was now her sister's door. The smell of smoke and soot stung her nostrils, and she recoiled in terror.

"TINA!" she screamed. But somehow she couldn't force herself to cross the threshold into the darkened room. Deep inside she knew she had to—her little sister was in danger—but instead she reeled back against the wall, helpless.

Suddenly the light in the room snapped on, and both of her parents were beside her.

"Brenda!" her mom cried, trying to hold her as Brenda squirmed away. "What's wrong, honey?"

"It's Tina!" Brenda screamed. "You've got to help her. Didn't you hear her? She needs our help!"

Her father grabbed her by the shoulders and gripped her hard.

"Brenda! Calm down! What are you talking about? Who is Tina?"

Brenda stopped. Her mouth dropped open and she stared at her parents as if they were total strangers.

"My sister," she finally whimpered. "My sister, Tina. Don't you remember? Don't you care? What's wrong with you? It's just like what happened with Ted. He disappeared from that room," she sobbed, pointing over the threshold into the awful place. "And you act like he never existed. Well, he was my brother. And Tina was my sister. And . . . " But Brenda couldn't go on. She broke into hysterical tears and let her father rock her gently in his arms.

"Brenda, sweetheart," her mother whispered. She was crying too. "You don't have a brother or a sister. You are an only child and you always have been. This is *our* room. It has been ever since we moved here."

Brenda twisted away, turned toward the open door, and caught her breath. Inside the room she could see her parents' bed and the big oak chest of drawers. From where she was, Brenda could see the photographs in their pretty frames, photos of her with her mom and dad . . . and no one else.

• • • • • • • • • • •

The sound of a car pulling up in the driveway woke Brenda. Slowly she opened her eyes and gazed at the early morning sunlight pooled on the rug beside her bed. With great effort, she drew herself up and walked groggily to the window. There was an old pickup truck in the driveway, and a small sedan that she didn't recognize was parked behind it. For a moment she just stood looking out, thinking that there was something she should know, but she couldn't quite figure out what. Something had happened, she was sure of it . . . but what?

Turning from the window, she called for her parents, but there was no answer. Then she heard the front door open and close downstairs.

"Mom?" she called tentatively. "Dad? Is that you?"

But there was no answer.

Thinking that they just hadn't heard her, she started to go downstairs when she felt a stab of fear. The voices downstairs were those of strangers! *Where are my parents?* Her mind raced. *Did they decide I was crazy and call these people to come get me?*

The door to the room at the end of the hall was closed. Cautiously Brenda eased to the head of the stairs. With her trembling hand just barely touching the rail, she leaned over to see who was there.

The foyer was still in shadow, but Brenda could make out two men standing just inside the front door.

"As you can see," the taller of the two said, "the fire didn't do much damage to the lower floor. The upper floor got the worst of it, and it was the smoke that got the family. Nice people, too," he added, shaking his head sadly. "They hadn't lived here all that long. Moved out from California."

Brenda felt her heart pounding. She glanced down at the railing under her shaking fingers and for the first time saw that it was charred and disintegrating. The wall behind her was scorched, and the smell of burnt wood hung in the damp air.

"Anybody know how the fire started, Luke?" the smaller man asked.

"Looks like it started in the big room at the end of the upstairs hall," the man named Luke responded. "You'll see for yourself when we go up. Nothing's been touched since it happened, and that was about five years ago."

"Why hasn't anyone been in to clean the place up?" The smaller man looked around. "Looks like it was a nice place."

"Oh, superstition," Luke answered. "Anybody who's been in here claimed to have heard crying coming from that room. Some say the place is haunted." He laughed. "My wife believes it, too. She says that when people die suddenly like that, sometimes the spirits can't accept what has happened. They stay on until something makes them realize that they're really dead."

It was as if a weight had been lifted. Suddenly aware of all she needed to know, Brenda turned and looked toward the room at the end of the hall. Now the door was standing open. Slowly she walked toward it.

Ted had been the first to accept it . . . then little Tina . . . and finally her parents. Now it was her turn to stop fighting it and accept what had happened. She stepped across the threshold—sad, but no longer afraid—and stood in the center of the room. Then Brenda took one last look at the faded blue flame-scarred walls and began to weep softly. She raised her hands to wipe the tears from her face and watched her flesh fading into thin air. Brenda cried sorrowfully as she slowly disappeared.

Downstairs, the small man held up his hand for the other to be quiet. "Did you hear that?" he said. "For a second I thought I heard someone crying."

"Oh, come on now. Don't tell me you're hearing things, too." Luke strained for a moment, then shook his head. "Nope. It's dead quiet."

It Waits

he photo on the front page of the local paper was dark and grainy, but the headline above it was very clear: SILVER BAY MONSTER CAUGHT ON FILM!

"Not much of a picture," Greg said to his friends Valerie and Andre. "The monster looks more like a big old log floating in the water."

Valerie shook her head. "And that's probably what it is," she agreed. "But the tourists eat it up."

"Yeah," Andre added. "Have you seen those stupid T-shirts with I SWAM IN SILVER BAY and a drawing of the monster munching on a swimmer?"

Greg nodded. He'd seen the T-shirts and the books, and even a dumb television show about the monster of Silver

Bay. The tale had been passed down for generations and could be traced back to an old Native American legend of a beast that came to feed near the shoreline when the waters were icy cold. Mr. Potter from the boathouse claimed that he had actually seen it at dusk three winters ago.

"It came up slow and easy," he'd said. "Then it moved a little closer to shore, like it was searching for something. Had long, sharp teeth, too. I could see them shining as it passed. I'll tell you this," Mr. Potter had added. "I'm glad I was onshore instead of in a boat, or I don't think I'd be here today."

Old Man Potter was known to tell a tall tale every now and then, but there were a few who were convinced that he was telling the truth. He'd described the monster in great detail as a gray-skinned beast about fifty feet long with an alligatorlike head. His description matched those of other sightings, but no one seemed to be able to get a good, clear photograph of the beast to prove that it really existed. Some said it lived most of the time deep in the bay where the water was always cold, only coming close to the surface in the fall or winter months.

"Well, thank goodness summer's over and all the tourists are going home," Valerie said walking away from the newsstand.

"Not all of them," Greg answered. "My cousin Mark and his folks are coming to visit from Arizona in a couple of weeks."

"I didn't know you had a cousin," Valerie said with interest. "How old is he? Is he nice?"

"Mean as can be," Greg said laughing. "And he looks a lot like the Silver Bay monster!"

• • • • • • • • • • •

Mark and his parents arrived just as the fall season set in. The leaves on the trees had turned brilliant shades of yellow, red, and orange, and the air was crisp and cool. It didn't take long for Greg and Mark to renew their friendship.

"You're so lucky to live here," Mark said as he and Greg stood on the porch overlooking the bay.

"Yeah," Greg agreed. "It's pretty, but it kind of gets boring sometimes. I think it would be really cool to live in a big city like Phoenix. You've got everything there."

Mark laughed. "We don't have any sea monsters."

"Neither do we," Greg said with a grin.

"What do you mean?" Mark questioned. I thought there was supposed to be some kind of monster here in Silver Bay, sort of like that Loch Ness thing in Scotland."

Greg shook his head. "That's just an old story."

Mark's voice took on a serious tone. "But I heard that quite a few people have vanished out on the bay."

"That's true, but the monster thing is just hype," Greg assured him. "Fall and winter conditions in the bay can be dangerous for boaters unless they really know how to handle it. The water is very cold and deep. If someone were to fall in and drown, that person's body would probably never be found. But," he added, "with all the tourists gone, the bay isn't so crowded now. This really is the best time to go out and have some fun." He looked at the early afternoon sunlight shimmering on the water. "Do you want to see for yourself? My buddy Andre has a boat. We could all go out for a sightseeing tour."

"But I thought you said it could be dangerous," Mark said hesitantly. "Are you sure your folks won't mind if we go?"

"It isn't risky if you know what you're doing, and we won't tell my folks," Greg said with a wink. "We'll just take a short trip and be back before supper time."

An hour later, Greg, Mark, Andre, and Valerie were cruising along in the small boat just off the shoreline.

"I'll take us around the point," Andre called out above the rumble of the outboard motor. He picked up speed and nosed the boat into deeper water.

Soon they rounded the long, tree-covered spit of land, entered a secluded cove, and turned back toward the shoreline, which was a tangle of trees and undergrowth that grew to the very edge of the water. Andre expertly guided them around a bare little islet that peeked just above the surface.

Greg pointed to the low, wide hump of sand. "That's Goose Bank," he explained. "At high tide it's underwater. People who don't know better get hung up on it sometimes. We have to stay in the channel here. It's a lot deeper."

"What about that over there?" Mark asked pointing to a spot a few hundred yards away. "Is that another bank?"

Greg turned to look. "What are you talking about?"

Mark shielded his eyes from the sun. "I guess I'm just seeing things," he said sheepishly. "It's gone."

"Maybe it was the creature," Andre offered with a grin. "This would be the perfect place for it . . . deep water . . . close to shore. Maybe we should get a better look. You have your camera with you, don't you Mark?"

"Stop teasing him," Valerie said with a shudder. "The monster is the last thing I would want to run into. Anyway, it's getting late. We should get back."

"She's right," Greg agreed.

"Oh, well," Andre said with mock disappointment. "Maybe next time I won't come out with a bunch of chickens." He started to turn the boat in a wide circle, but suddenly it stopped with a jolt and the motor died.

"Oh no," Greg moaned. "You didn't hit the bank, did you?"

"No, I didn't hit the bank," Andre said, scowling. "There must be something floating. Maybe its a log or . . . "

"Look!" Valerie cried out before he could finish. "There *is* something in the water."

The four watched in fear as a dark shadow circled slowly under the boat.

Greg leaned away from the edge of the boat. "No, there're no sharks. Andre, you'd better get the motor started."

"Right," Andre said quietly. He yanked firmly on the starter cable once . . . twice . . . and even a third time. On the fourth pull the motor finally sputtered to life, and as it did, the water a few feet away started to bubble and churn.

"Something's stirring up the water!" Valerie called out nervously. "Let's get out of here!"

All at once something huge broke the surface.

"YEEEAAAGGGGGGGHHHHHHH!!" Andre screamed as an enormous scaly head rose into the air, causing a wave of cold water to slosh over the edge of the boat, drenching everything and killing the motor.

In a panic Andre stood to get a better grip on the starter cable, causing the little boat to sway violently. Suddenly he was pitched into the dark green water, and the monster instantly submerged. Then everything was dead quiet except for the wavelets slapping against the side of the rocking boat.

"We've got to help him!" Valerie cried. But there wasn't a ripple in the water, and the kids were too afraid to jump in.

"Andre's gone," Greg said flatly. "The monster really *does* exist."

Mark gazed down wide-eyed at the water. "What are we going to do?" he whimpered.

Without answering, Greg slid toward the motor and tried the starter cable a few times. "The motor's flooded," he said finally. "We're not going anywhere."

Valerie looked toward shore. "All we have to do is wait. Someone will come looking for us," she said hopefully.

Greg shook his head. "No one saw us take the boat and nobody knows where we are."

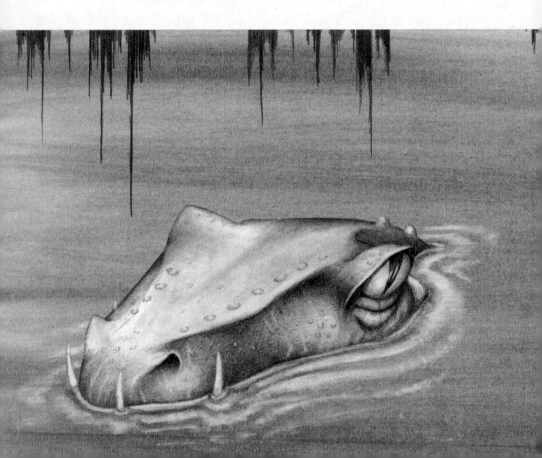

"Well, we can't just *sit* here," Mark said, trying hard to control the trembling in his voice. "What if that thing comes back? We're soaking wet. We'll freeze to death if we stay out here all night."

"Mark's right," Greg answered. "We're going to have to try to swim for it. It's only a hundred yards or so to shore."

"Are you out of your mind?"

"We're no safer in the boat," Greg yelled. "Swimming to shore is our only chance."

"Well, I won't do it!" Valerie insisted. "I'd rather freeze. I won't get in the water with that . . . that *thing* out there."

Greg looked at Mark. "We can make it," he said with determination. "I'm going to go for it. Are you with me?"

Shaking with fright and cold, Mark finally nodded, and the two boys slowly eased themselves over the edge of the boat. Then as quietly as they could, they headed toward shore.

The water was painfully cold, but Greg willed his body to keep moving, his eyes fixed on the shoreline. They hadn't gotten but a few yards when they heard Valerie scream. The two boys looked back and saw the water swirling around the tiny boat. Suddenly it was tossed into the air. It landed upside down on the surface with a resounding slap, and Valerie tried to clamber up onto it. But something unseen gripped her flailing legs and tugged her forcefully under the surface.

"Swim!" Greg shouted to his cousin. But it was too late. The water was already growing darker beneath them and in front of them. Something was between them and the shoreline.

"It's out there," Mark cried. "We—" But before he could finish, he disappeared.

Greg began to swim with every bit of energy he had. His arms churned across the surface, until all at once he felt something solid beneath his feet. Crying hard, he dragged himself onto the shore and looked around. "Oh, no!" he wailed. He had made it to land all right . . . but to Goose Bank. The tide was rising, and soon the bank—and Greg— would be totally submerged.

As the waves lapped closer to his feet, Greg called for help. But there was no one to hear him . . . no one but *it*.

The Roadside Attraction

ulianne thumbed through the magazine she had been reading in the backseat of the family car. On the final page she found what she wanted. It was a listing of fun magic paraphernalia to send away for. Julianne loved magic, and she loved to astonish her friends. She was just starting to fill out the order form when her mother asked if she was hungry.

Julianne nodded. "Yeah, I could go for something to eat."

"Well, I could sure use a break," her dad chimed in from the driver's seat. "I need to stretch my legs."

It was a long drive home from Yosemite to Chicago, and they still had hours to go. As they looked for the next exit, they passed a billboard that announced SEE THE AMAZING ALIEN BEAST AT THE RIVER RUN DINER AND TRADING POST. NEXT EXIT.

"Let's stop there," Julianne pleaded.

Her parents glanced at each other, then her father flipped on the turn signal. "Well, at least if the food's lousy we can have a good laugh at the Amazing Alien Beast," he said chuckling as he eased the car toward the exit ramp.

The diner was shaped like a huge stone teepee with glass doors. Two smaller teepees stood on either side. The one on the right was the trading post, while the one on the left was a performance area with a sign outside listing show times.

"Looks like we're just in time for the last show," her dad said as he ushered Julianne and her mom toward the building on the left. "Afterward, we can get a bite to eat in the diner."

The inside walls were draped with velvety red curtains, and several rows of chairs faced a small stage.

"Have a seat wherever you like, folks," offered a small red-haired man in jeans and a faded cowboy shirt. "Alonzo the Great will be appearing any minute now."

Julianne noticed that the man emphasized the word *appearing*, and she had visions of a mysterious man in a dark cape materializing before them in a puff of smoke. Sitting in the front row with her parents, she looked around. There were only five other people in the audience. The lights dimmed and Julianne heard her mom gasp. A costumed figure was standing in the spotlight just as she'd imagined—seemingly out of thin air.

The couple behind her applauded politely, and the man onstage bowed. "Thank you," he said in a slightly distorted voice.

"Great makeup job," Julianne's dad whispered.

"He looks positively out of this world," her mom agreed.

40

With a protruding canine snout and elongated ears that arched upward, the man was made up to look like some sort of wolf-being. His eyes were pale gold, and when he smiled he showed a set of slightly pointed teeth. A soft coat of fine gray fur covered his face.

"I am but a visitor to your dimension," the actor began dramatically. "Here in your world some of my powers seem magical, but I assure you I am merely a performer—a magician, nothing more."

With that, he pulled a large bouquet of fake flowers from his sleeve, which brought a smattering of applause. Julianne raised an eyebrow. *Boring*, she thought.

"You are all very kind," the magician said, then turned his gaze directly on Julianne as if reading her mind. "But I have a feeling that you might like to see something more spectacular. So be it."

He moved gracefully to a table. On it were a few items: a colorful ball, a framed photo, a book, and a small bowl of water with a goldfish circling lazily inside it. With a flourish, he passed his "paw" over the table and wiggled his fingers, each of which ended in a curved, tapered claw.

Must be some kind of gloves, Julianne thought. *Nobody could grow nails like that.*

"Watch carefully, my friends," he advised in his peculiar, rhythmic tone. "You will be amazed."

Suddenly Julianne became aware of an unusual, sweet scent in the air, and she forgot about everything except what was happening on the small stage. There, right before her eyes, the items were fading from view one by one . . . very slowly. First the ball disappeared, then the photo and book

41

followed. Finally the fishbowl vanished, leaving the goldfish swimming in mid air. Then it, too, disappeared.

No one made a sound.

"Please, my friend," the magician said, gesturing to a heavyset man sitting near the door. "Come and see for yourself that your eyes are not deceiving you."

The man stood and lumbered onto the stage. He ran his hand over the table, then looked closely at the floor underneath for trapdoors or mirrors.

"I'll be darned," he said, rubbing the back of his neck. "They sure are gone! How did you do that?"

The magician smiled, exposing sharp teeth. "I assure you," he said, "the items are all residing safely in my own dimension. In fact," he added with a wink, "at this very moment there is an audience *there* that is just as surprised to see the objects appear as you were to see them go."

Everyone laughed, but Julianne felt a creepy tingle down to her toes. There was something strange about the magician, who was now raising his hand with a flourish and giving a short bow to more enthusiastic applause.

"Thank you, one and all!" the magician said grandly.

"OK, folks," the red-haired man in jeans called from where he stood near the door. "Now the griddle is hot, the trading post is open, and we'd be quite pleased if you'd join us. But first," he added, motioning toward the stage, "you're welcome to take a look around."

Julianne, who had turned with the rest of the audience to listen to the man, looked back to the stage only to find that the magician had vanished.

"That's quite an act," her dad said as they walked toward

the diner, "though the bit about the other dimension is a little weird. Still I wonder why the guy is working in this little out-of-the-way place. It seems as if he could do better."

In the diner Julianne picked at her tuna sandwich, no longer hungry. All she could think about was the magician's act. *I'll never be that good of a magician*, she thought, *unless . . .*

"Excuse me," she said to her parents. "I'm going to find the rest room. I think it's outside."

But once outside Julianne headed away from the ladies room, hurried to the performance area, and ducked inside. Now that it was empty, the place had an extra-eerie quality about it. Julianne took a deep breath. She could still smell the sweet scent she had detected earlier. Walking around the room, she ran her fingers along the crimson curtain.

"I wonder where this goes?" she mumbled as she parted the curtain and saw a tiny passageway behind it. A light shone from a small room at the end. Creeping quietly along the passageway, she reached the lighted area and peeked in just in time to see the magician spray himself from head to toe with a dull red fluid that came from a crystal container. Instantly the familiar sweet scent she'd smelled in the performance area flooded the room. The magician set the container on a low shelf, and then faded from sight!

For a moment Julianne wrestled with a sudden urge that came over her. She *had* to have that spray. Quickly stepping into the room, she tiptoed toward the container and had just laid her hand on it when . . .

"What are you doing here?" the small red-haired man demanded angrily. He was the one who had announced the performance.

43

Julianne turned to face him. "I . . . I was looking for the rest room," she said finally. Her thoughts were spinning. Could he see what she was up to?

The man stared at her for a moment and then said, "I don't like people snooping around my place. The rest room is in the main building. Now get outta here!"

"Uh, sorry," she replied, smiling weakly. Then as the man turned away, she slipped the crystal container into her pocket and raced back to the diner.

• • • • • • • • • • •

"Wow!" Jake Taylor exclaimed when Julianne made a glass of orange juice disappear for several of her friends at school. They hadn't believed she could really do it, but with the small crystal container tucked secretly in her palm, Julianne simply needed to wave her hand over the juice and . . . poof!

"How did you *do* that?" Jake asked, obviously impressed.

"Oh," Julianne answered coyly. "It's just something I picked up from a colleague while I was on the road."

"Does it work on people?" Jake's sister Karen asked.

"I suppose," Julianne responded thoughtfully. She remembered watching as the magician faded from sight. "Maybe I'll show you that tomorrow."

Later that night, Julianne paced sleeplessly in her room. "It would be the best trick in the whole world," she muttered under her breath. "Imagine me actually making a live person vanish into thin air!" She picked up the crystal container, then set it down on her dresser once again. *But what if it really*

does work? she thought. She saw the magician make things disappear, but she didn't see him make things reappear. How could she be certain she could bring a person back?

Suddenly Julianne heard her dog scratching at her door. "Come on in, Jericho," she said, letting her small terrier into the room. He immediately scurried after a tiny cricket that had been hiding in the shadows in the corner of the room. The insect leaped to the safety of the windowsill.

All at once, Julianne had an idea. *I'll test it on the cricket*, she thought, directing the vial in the direction of the little creature and spraying. Unfortunately it was precisely at the same moment that her dog decided to jump up, and the brick-red liquid covered Jericho's dark brown fur.

"Oh no!" Julianne cried sweeping Jericho into her arms. But as she held him, Jericho slowly faded. Then, all at once, he was gone.

"What have I done?" she sobbed. And then she threw herself on the bed and cried herself to sleep.

• • • • • • • • • • •

When she woke in the morning, Julianne rubbed her red, swollen eyes. "It's all my fault," she whimpered, gazing sadly at the empty dog bed in the corner of her room. She started to turn away but stopped when she noticed a dim shadow in the center of Jericho's blanket. As she watched, the shadow slowly took shape until Jericho reappeared.

"You're back!" she exclaimed, hugging the bewildered dog. "The effect must wear off on living things!"

The dog gave her a confused glance, then curled up on the floor and began to lick its fur.

Julianne picked up the container. "I've got to do this before I lose my nerve. Here goes," she said with a smile, and directed the spray toward herself.

For a moment she felt sick to her stomach, like she did when she rode the whirligig at the fair. Everything around her was hazy and hot. She gasped for air and tried to focus her eyes. Slowly . . . slowly . . . a strange room began to come into view. She was on some sort of raised platform, and there was a spotlight shining down on her. She tried to see into the shadows beyond. There were lots of people sitting in rows of seats and they were all . . . screaming!

She took a step toward them, and a small child in the front row began to cry. But it wasn't like any child she had ever seen before. As her vision cleared Julianne saw that it had wolflike features, yellow eyes, and a mouthful of tiny sharp teeth. Soft gray fur covered its face and hands.

"What is going on here?" she shrieked. "Where am I?"

All at once someone gripped her firmly by the arm and tugged her to a curtained room near the stage.

"I knew this would happen," a wolflike man said in a distorted voice. Julianne stared in astonishment.

"You're the magician from the diner," she whimpered. "What is this place? What are those . . . those . . . creatures out there? They acted like I was some kind of monster. I want to go home."

"I was afraid of this," he said softly, ignoring her questions. "When I returned to your dimension and found the bottle missing, I knew someone had stolen the potion and it would only be a matter of time. Then when the objects started coming through . . . I knew for certain. Now we'll just have to find something to do with you."

"How long does it take before this stuff wears off?" Julianne demanded.

"It doesn't wear off," he said finally.

"That's not true!" she shouted. "I tried it on my dog and he came back. I saw it happen."

"Listen carefully," he said slowly. "That potion is a well-protected secret used by magicians in my dimension. We amaze audiences by making strange things *appear* before their eyes. There are many dimensions to visit, but I chose yours. I can go back and forth as those of my kind can, but objects and other living things, including humans, from your dimension can go only one way. I cannot send you back."

"But my *dog*," Julianne wailed. Then all of a sudden she looked at the magician's soft fur, glanced deeply into his golden wolf eyes and realized the truth. "He . . . he's like you. That's why. The potion works for you and for him, because you're so alike." Her shoulders shook with sobs as she understood what had happened—that she was trapped in another dimension with no hope of going back to her own.

The magician placed his paw on her shoulder. "I'm sorry," he growled softly. "But you brought it on yourself. Still, we will find a place for you here. In fact, I think you will make a fine attraction. We can bill you as the Amazing Alien Being at a little roadside house not too far from here. It is an out-of-the-way place, and no one will ask any questions. Yes, you'll make a fine roadside attraction, my dear. A fine one, indeed!"

The Rocking Horse

miling, Jason ran his fingers over the freshly sanded wood. He liked the way it felt, so smooth and warm.

"You just need to take a little more off that edge," his grandfather said. "When we're done, this will be an end table fit for a queen." He grinned from ear to ear. "A queen like your grandmother."

"OK, Gramps," Jason said as he went back to work on the raw wood with the sandpaper. His grandfather was one of the best woodworkers he'd ever seen, and Jason was glad to learn his grandfather's talents. He loved woodworking, and was getting really good at it. Ever since his parents had been killed in a car accident ten months ago, he and his little sister, Sarah, had been living with their grandparents out in the country. So Jason had gotten to spend a lot of time in the workshop with his grandfather.

The first couple of months after the accident had been hard on Jason, but they had been even more difficult for Sarah. Their grandparents were living on a pension and could barely afford to provide for themselves, let alone feed and clothe two kids. There was little money left over for extras.

Like birthday presents, Jason thought to himself, as he sanded the leg of the table.

Sarah's fifth birthday was in a month. It would be the first one she would celebrate without their mom and dad, and Jason knew it was up to him to try to help his sister cope with their absence.

"Gramps," he said, looking up. "I've been thinking about Sarah's birthday."

His grandfather nodded. "Me, too. Your sister can't seem to talk about anything else . . . unless she's talking about that fancy rocking horse in the window of Samuelson's Toy Shop."

"Well, I want to do something special for her," Jason said, "and since the horse in the toy shop is more than a hundred dollars, I thought if you had some extra wood, I'd just make her one."

Jason's grandpa smiled and put his hand on the boy's shoulder. "That's a really nice idea. I could help you if you like."

"Thanks, but no, Grandpa. I'd like to do it myself."

"I understand," the elderly man said, proud that his grandson wanted to test his own skills. "Let's finish up here, and then we'll see what we can find in the woodpile for your sister's horse."

• • • • • • • • • • •

Three weeks later, Jason was nearly finished with the parts for the rocking horse, but he still needed to assemble it.

"More pie?" his grandmother asked just as he was leaving the dinner table to go back out to the workshop.

"No thanks, Grandma," he answered. "I've got to finish up what I'm working on."

"What *are* you working on?" she asked curiously. "You've been spending every night out there lately."

"It's a secret," Jason said, winking at his grandfather.

"I think he's making something for me," Sarah blurted out. "It's something for my birthday, isn't it?"

Jason just grinned at her. "You'll just have to wait and see."

Once in the workshop, Jason frowned as he studied the parts that he had cut and finished so carefully. Everything was ready to assemble and paint, but he still needed a good-sized length of hardwood to make the connecting pegs, the rockers, and the handles at the horse's head. Then he had an idea. Grabbing a handsaw, he stepped out into the summer night.

The full moon shone overhead, lighting Jason's way as he cut across the field and headed for the old cemetery. Shivering in spite of the warm night, he stopped at the low iron gate.

"Chill out," he muttered to himself. "You've been here a hundred times during the day."

It was true; Jason had to walk by the place on his way home from school. No one had been buried there for quite a while, and the longer the place stayed untended, the creepier it became. From where he stood, Jason could see the gnarled trunk and bare branches of the old tree he had in mind for Sarah's rocking horse. Its dark shape stood out against the sky, towering a few feet from a large raised tomb topped with a small stone angel.

"It'll be perfect," he said aloud, trying to build up his nerve. "Nobody will miss some wood from this old place."

Not the type to frighten easily, Jason couldn't help feeling that there was something particularly unsettling about the cemetery. It was as though something was waiting in there, actually listening for his next move. But Sarah's birthday was only three days away, and Jason knew that if he didn't get the wood cut tonight, he wouldn't get the horse done in time. Gripping the top rail, he hoisted himself over the gate and dropped down in the soft dirt of the cemetery.

Suddenly something rustled in the shadow of a nearby headstone, and Jason froze. All at once some sort of large animal broke cover and raced toward a gap in the fence.

Just an old raccoon, he thought, sighing heavily. *I'd better get what I came for and get out of here.*

Running his hands over the dark wood of the old tree, Jason peeled back the bark here and there, then chose a slender branch. Carefully he began to saw, and as the serrated teeth bit into the dead wood, Jason thought he felt a slight shudder run through the branch. "No way," he muttered to himself and continued cutting.

He was nearly finished when he suddenly had the uncomfortable feeling of being watched. Turning slightly, Jason saw a figure above him. He gasped and almost screamed, but then he caught himself.

"Get it together, Jason!" he scolded himself. What he'd seen was only the stone angel from the nearby tomb. In the moonlight he could see its cold, pale face staring at him. Shrugging, Jason turned back to the tree and sawed faster. Within seconds the branch gave way with a pitiful crack. Hoisting it onto his shoulder, he started to leave but caught the toe of his sneaker on something and fell heavily to the ground.

Rolling onto one side, Jason realized that he had tripped over part of a tree root. He also noticed that several twisted roots appeared to have grown toward the aged tomb.

He studied the roots and saw that the tips disappeared under the tomb's pitted gray wall. A carved stone over the rusted gate bore the name of the person inside.

"Mary Elizabeth Drew," he read. "1904 to 1909." *How sad*, he thought. *She was just Sarah's age when she died.* Quickly scrambling to his feet, Jason headed for the workshop where he quickly went to work on finishing Sarah's horse.

But as he slowly worked the wood, he became aware of an eerie sensation: The branch felt warm, almost as if it were alive.

• • • • • • • • • • •

"Why, it's beautiful!" Jason's grandmother exclaimed when Jason brought the finished rocking horse into the house two evenings later. Sarah had been so anxious for her birthday to arrive that she had gone to bed early, giving the family a chance to make the final preparations for the small party they were throwing for her.

"Thanks," Jason responded proudly. "I thought that instead of wrapping it, I would just put it out here in the dining room so she can see it as soon as she gets up."

His grandfather nodded. "That's a great idea. Sarah is very lucky to have a brother as thoughtful as you."

"She sure is," his grandmother agreed, walking over to the horse and tying a large red bow around its neck. "There, now I think we're ready. Maybe we should all get a good night's sleep so we can keep up with Sarah tomorrow!"

Once in bed, Jason fell quickly asleep, but awoke a few hours later to the distant rumble of his grandfather's snoring. He smiled, wondering how anyone could sleep through it. *Grandma and Grandpa are both lucky they're hard of hearing*, he thought, his eyes getting droopy. But suddenly he snapped them open again. It was like something gently rocking back and forth on the hardwood floor of the dining room.

Had Sarah gotten up early and found her present? Quietly Jason tiptoed down the stairs. He peered into the darkened dining room. No one was there, the sound had stopped, and the rocking horse stood near the large bay window exactly as he had left it hours ago. Shaking his head, Jason returned to his room, but he couldn't dismiss the feeling that something wasn't quite right.

• • • • • • • • • • •

"Wow!" Sarah shrieked excitedly when she ran downstairs the next morning and laid eyes on Jason's present. "It's the most beautiful rocking horse in the whole world!" She threw her arms around her older brother, giving him a big hug, then dashed to her steed.

Jason felt good as he watched her stroke the golden yarn mane and tail. "Go ahead," he coaxed. "Try it out."

She climbed onto the slightly curved wooden seat that served as a saddle and began to rock back and forth, while Jason and their grandparents enjoyed her happiness. But suddenly a shiver passed through Jason when he realized that the sound of the horse moving on the floor was the same sound he had heard the night before. Quickly he told himself it was just his imagination, wanting to hold onto the joyous moment with his family.

After breakfast Sarah opened her other presents, but the horse was clearly her favorite. She even dragged it onto the porch when she went outside to play, and Jason noticed her sitting beside it, chattering away.

"Are you talking to your horse?" Jason asked stepping out onto the porch.

"Of course not," she answered, as if he had asked a very silly question. "I'm talking to my friend. It's her turn to ride it."

Jason looked at the empty saddle and back to his sister. "Oh, yeah? What's your friend's name?" he asked with a grin.

"Mary Elizabeth," she answered happily.

Jason looked at her in stunned surprise. That was the name he had read on the tomb in the cemetery.

That night Jason was awakened once again by the rocking sound, but this time it was coming from Sarah's room. He slipped from bed and tiptoed quietly to her door. He could hear voices inside . . . Sarah's and . . . who else's? Slowly he turned the knob and pushed open the door. What he saw made his heart feel as if it would pound right out of his chest. Sarah was standing beside her rocking horse, and seated in the saddle was the shimmering form of a little girl. She was dressed in a long, old-fashioned nightgown.

The phantom slowly moved to Sarah's side and glared at Jason. Its eyes glowed angrily. "She is my friend," it warned in a soft, hollow voice. "We are going to be together forever."

It took Sarah's small hand in its own translucent one and began to lead her toward the door. Sarah did not protest.

"No!" Jason shouted. He lunged for Sarah, but before he could move, something twisted around his ankles, making him fall to the floor. In terror, he saw what gripped him. It was several long, writhing tendrils that had sprouted from the wooden horse!

In panic, Jason cried out for his grandparents, knowing they would not hear him. He watched helplessly as the two children—one human, one not—stepped out of the room. "Sarah!" he cried, his mind racing. Then grabbing the lamp cord that ran along the wall, he tugged hard. A heavy brass lamp tumbled from the nightstand and crashed to the floor. Jason picked it up and began to chop at the slender tendrils. Struggling free, he scrambled to his feet and dashed out onto the porch.

The moon was waning and the landscape was bathed in long, dark shadows. Although he couldn't see his sister, Jason knew where the specter would lead her . . . and he knew what he had to do. He raced back into the house, grabbed a flashlight and a box of wooden matches from the fireplace mantel, then headed for the abandoned cemetery.

Moments later he found himself in front of the old stone tomb. Fighting back his fear, Jason stepped into the dank, forbidding crypt. Sarah was huddled in a corner. She seemed to be in a trance, wrapped in tree roots that trailed under the wall of the tomb. "Sarah?" he whispered as he

56

tried to take a step toward her. But it was as if she were on the other side of a curtain that he could not push away . . . a curtain between life and death.

"It will be over soon. She is mine now," a mournful voice said softly. "You cannot reach her."

Jason watched the roots move toward his sister's small throat, and then he remembered the box of wooden matches he gripped in his hand.

"Please work," he begged. But his hands were shaking so badly that he dropped the first match. Luckily the second one flared to life, and he held the long fireplace match under one of the horrible tree roots until it went up into flames.

Suddenly the tree seemed to scream as smoke billowed toward the night sky, and Jason was relieved to find that the roots had dropped away from around his sister.

He lifted Sarah to her feet, and as he began to lead her from the crypt, the ghost child blocked his way.

"You cannot take her!" it shrieked. "She is mine!"

"That's where you're wrong!" Jason screamed back. "Your link to this world is going up in flames." Gathering his courage, he pulled Sarah out of the crypt, and the two raced out of the cemetery without looking back.

By dawn the ashes had cooled. As the sun rose above the horizon, there was no one to watch as several small buds unfurled amid the charred remains of the tree. Only the stone angel stared mutely as tiny new roots inched through the ground toward the tomb.

Cave Dwellers

rian and his friends Tony, Hillary, and Richard stepped from the darkened theater into the brightly lit lobby. "That was really cool!" Brian exclaimed as he and the others stopped to look at a movie poster on the wall beside the entrance.

In the suspenseful scene, a world-famous archaeologist and his three student assistants were uncovering a pair of dusty, ancient scrolls from a hidden compartment in an eerie old tomb. Several shadowy figures were lurking in the background, as if ready to cause some trouble.

"Yeah, it was a cool movie," Tony agreed. "But if I had been one of the assistants, I would never have let those old guys steal the scrolls without a fight."

"Come on," Hillary said. "The zombie creatures had them surrounded. They *had* to give up the scrolls."

Brian frowned. "I think Tony's right. It would have been better if they'd tried to fight their way out in the first place. Then they wouldn't have had to face the zombies later."

Hillary rolled her eyes. "Then there wouldn't have been much of a movie."

Richard hadn't said a word. In fact, he was still staring at the poster as if lost in thought. "You know what would really be cool?" he finally uttered wishfully. "If *we* could go on a dig in some ancient tomb or something."

"Well, you're out of luck," Tony said, laughing. "There're no tombs around here."

"No, but we could explore Spirit Cave," Hillary pointed out.

"But a cave isn't the same as a tomb," Tony replied.

"Well, I read in a magazine that about twenty years ago some people were exploring down south in Mammoth Caves, and they found a mummy," Hillary said.

Richard snickered and rolled his eyes. "Give me a break."

"Cross my heart," Hillary shot back.

"She's right," Brian said. "It wasn't like an Egyptian mummy or anything, but it was a body of some guy who died hundreds of years ago. Nobody's ever found anything as cool as that in the caves up around here, but Mr. Glaser, my next-door neighbor who studies history, told me that Native Americans in this area used the caves right at the ridge of County Line Park for all kinds of things."

"Like what?" Richard asked with interest. He and his family had only recently moved to Kentucky, and he didn't know a lot about the area.

"They stored food there. And the shamans—they're kind of like priests—they sometimes would perform secret rituals supposedly to trap evil spirits."

"What kind of evil spirits?" Hillary questioned. Brian's story had mesmerized the circle of friends.

"Well, Mr. Glaser told me about half-man, half-bat creatures that could make themselves invisible."

"Sounds cool," Tony commented.

"That's not what the local Native Americans thought," Brian said. "These bat creatures supposedly captured people."

"What for?" Richard asked with a shiver.

Brian shrugged. "Nobody knows for sure, but their victims were never seen alive again. The legend says that the shamans tracked the creatures to their hiding place in a cave then used magic to seal them in." Brian's eyes widened as an idea occurred to him. "Why don't we go see if Mr. Glaser's story has truth to it?"

Tony shook his head. "But lots of kids have already explored Spirit Cave to death."

"Who cares?" Brian said eagerly. "I'll bet there's still some cool arrowheads and stuff up there, and it's close enough so we can just ride our bikes!"

It didn't take long for him to convince the others. They decided to set out on their expedition on the weekend.

• • • • • • • • • • •

On Saturday morning Brian checked the batteries in his flashlight and made room in his backpack for a few extra granola bars. Satisfied that he had everything he needed, he hopped on his bike and headed toward Hillary's house. When he got there she was already waiting at the end of her block with Richard and Tony.

"My mom wasn't going to let me go," she said breathlessly. "I had to swear to be back by lunchtime. Let's get out of here before she changes her mind."

County Line Park was a grassy oasis on the border of a sparse forest of maple and beech trees. Underlying the forest was a layer of limestone. Over thousands of years, groundwater had seeped through the limestone, scouring out caves and channels within.

"We'll have to hike up from here," Brian explained to Richard as he secured his bike cable around a tree. "There's a cave near the top of the hill. That's where my dad and I found all those arrowheads."

Ten minutes later the group stood at the narrow cave entrance. Richard shined his flashlight inside. "Has anybody ever gotten lost in there?" he asked nervously.

"No," Brian assured him. "Spirit Cave doesn't go back very far. A couple of passages lead off it, but they're both dead ends. If it's bat people you're worried about, forget it. This cave doesn't even have any real bats."

"Real bats?" Richard asked in surprise.

"Sure," Tony answered. "There are zillions of them around here. But they're plain old brown bats. They won't hurt you or anything. You just don't want to scare a whole bunch of them inside of a cave, because they start flying all over."

"Hey, you guys!" Hillary called. "I don't want to waste time out here. Let's see what we can find."

One by one, the others slipped inside the low, wide chamber, which was dim and cool in spite of the sunny day. Richard moved the slender beam of his flashlight across the sandy floor.

"From the tracks, it looks like this place has been well explored," he said disappointedly. "We won't find anything."

"Look!" Tony said with mock pride. "I've already made a discovery." He held a crushed soda can in the glow of his light.

"What's this?" Richard asked, ignoring him. He pointed his light toward a smaller opening.

"One of the passages," Hillary answered, heading off along the dark, rocky corridor. "Come on, I'll show you."

The others followed her lead. After a few moments she called back a warning. "Watch where you're stepping," she grumbled. "The ground's not very even in here."

But Hillary's warning came too late for Richard, who stumbled over a furrow in the path and dropped his flashlight. It rolled into the shadows at the far edge of the corridor and lodged in a crevice between two slabs of rock.

"I'll get it," Tony offered, trotting over to it. But as he turned Richard's flashlight to pick it up, he noticed that the beam lit up something beyond the passage wall. Two light-colored slabs of limestone with odd markings scratched into them covered most of the gap. "There's an opening here," he said excitedly. "It looks like somebody put these rocks here on purpose, but they're a little loose." He motioned to his friends. "Come here, you guys. Help me."

"Wait a minute," Brian cautioned. "Those look like some sort of ancient petroglyphs on the slabs. Maybe we shouldn't mess with this until someone who knows what they're doing checks it out."

"We're just going to take a look," Tony said. "C'mon. If it looks dangerous, we'll put the rocks back over the opening and let somebody else know about it."

With a hesitant shrug, Brian agreed. Working together, the four kids were able to roll the two limestone slabs out of the way, exposing a wide gap big enough to crawl into.

Hillary knelt at the edge of the opening and leaned over. "Brrrrrrr, the air in here is so cold and musty," she said as a small shower of sand and pebbles streamed in, dusting her hands with a fine, thin coating of limestone. She turned her flashlight from one angle to another.

"I hear running water," she said. "Let's check it out."

"Maybe we should go back—" Brian began.

"Come on, Brian," Tony interrupted. "This might be what we were looking for. I don't want anybody else to get to it first."

"Tony's right," Richard agreed. "I say we check it out."

Squeezing through the gap, the kids found themselves at the top of a wide rock ledge in a cavern wall. Almost like a steep ramp jutting out from the rock wall, the ledge sloped steadily down about thirty feet to the floor of a very large cavern. The moist, rocky walls all around them had a slight greenish glow that was just bright enough to enable the group to see their surroundings.

"I've heard about stuff that glows in caves," Brian whispered as they made their way carefully down the steep ledge to the floor of the cavern. "It's some kind of fungus or something."

Tony held his hand up. "Listen. Did you hear that? I heard some squeaking. I'll bet there are bats in here." He turned his flashlight to the cavern roof, but saw only bare rock.

"Look!" Richard cried, pointing the beam of his flashlight toward a large boulder near the opposite wall. The huge rock was covered with primitive markings. A small, swift stream of water ran in a channel beside it. "There's your running water, Hillary. It must be an underground stream. It seems to be seeping in from an opening about halfway up the wall, then it disappears into that tunnel. It probably goes back underground. And look." He played the beam of his light across the entrances to several passageways that led off from the main cavern. "This place must be riddled with tunnels and caverns that no one knows about. Just think—because of a freak accident with my flashlight, we'll be the first to explore them!"

Creeping across the cavern floor, Richard examined the wall beside the big rock. The damp, glistening surface was inscribed with the same strange markings as the boulder. All at once he gasped and backed up, bumping into Brian. Both boys fell to the soft earth right at the foot of a crude statue carved right into the rock wall. Its large, evil face stared directly down at them, and its hideous eyes shone with the reflected gleam of Brian's flashlight.

"It's . . . it's a statue of a monster, just like the ones in the local Native American legend," Brian said with a shudder. The body appeared almost human, but a pair of batlike wings rose behind it, and its long fingers were tipped with hooked claws. The scowling mouth of the stone creature was open, and crystal clear water bubbled out over its sharp stone teeth, then trickled down the body, forming a pool at the statue's feet before flowing away into the darkness beyond.

"Wow!" Hillary marveled as she looked up at the statue. "It's incredible! Somebody must have thought this place was really important to go to all the work of carving this." She reached out her cupped hand and let it fill with water.

"I wouldn't do that if I were you," Brian cautioned. "My guess is that this statue was carved by shamans as a warning about something. Maybe the water. Maybe it's poison."

"Oh, come on," she answered. "The streams around here are OK to drink." She lifted her hand to her lips and took a sip. "It's good." Her voice echoed slightly.

"Listen to that," Richard said smiling. "There's an echo." He raised his head and called out, "Hellooooo." His greeting vibrated eerily through the chamber.

"Don't do that," Brian begged. He fought a sudden urge to race out of the cave. "I have a bad feeling about this place. Look, now we know what's down here, so let's just—"

But before he could finish, Richard cupped both hands around his mouth, threw back his head, and called out an even louder "Hellllooooooooooooo."

All at once the cavern filled with a whirling sound, and then the air seemed to boil and surge with the beating of hundreds of small, unseen wings.

"What's happening?" Hillary cried. Something invisible struck her cheek, leaving a long scratch. A droplet of blood welled up below her eye and trickled down to her mouth.

Richard fell to the floor and covered his face, while Tony crouched in a corner. Pinned against the slimy wall, Brian felt pokes and jabs coming at him from every side as the squealing noise rose all around him to a frenzied pitch. It was happening so fast. All he could do was lash out at the

66

invisible winged creatures racing back and forth, casting frightening shadows across the walls of the cavern.

Finally the fury subsided, and the cavern grew quiet. "What was *that*?" Hillary moaned as she dabbed cool water from the stream on her injured cheek. Then she jumped back with a shriek. "There's something in this water!"

Brian looked down and saw that she was right. Something was struggling to stay afloat in the pool of water that rippled at the feet of the statue. At first all he could see was the movement. Then slowly a shadow began to form, and at last a small brown bat became visible. It labored to the edge of the pool, then flew upward to nestle in the shadows of the cavern roof.

Brian looked at Richard sternly. "Do *not* yell in here again," he said, glancing upward at the seemingly bare roof. "There must be hundreds of bats up there. *We* just can't see *them*. And if we can't see them, who knows what else might be in here."

"Invisible bats? But how did they become invisible?" Tony asked with a tremor in his voice.

"The air maybe?" Brian answered.

"Or the water!" Richard rasped, pointing at Hillary.

To everyone's amazement, their friend was fading. With a sob, she held up her hands. "You—you can see right through me!" she said with a gasp, looking at Brian in bewilderment. Suddenly Brian saw that she wasn't looking at him, but *beyond* him. Her expression was turning from confusion to one of complete panic.

"Get away!" she screamed, snapping her horrified gaze from side to side. Cringing, she shouted in horror, "Stay away!"

"The water," Brian yelled as his friend disappeared completely. He reached out for her, and although he could still feel her, she just wasn't there. "Quick, Hillary! Get into the water!" he demanded, forcing her toward the pool. "Drinking the water probably made you invisible, just like the bats. One of them reappeared when it got soaked in the pool. Maybe the same thing will work for you."

"It's working," Tony whispered in awe, as Hillary landed in the water and slowly became visible again. And as she did, the boys could see that her face was twisted into a grimace of sheer terror.

"They're all around us!" she wailed, clutching Brian. "Those things—" She stabbed her finger in the air toward the carved stone statue. "I could only see them when I was invisible! They're everywhere!"

"We've got to get out of here!" Richard yelled.

Suddenly Brian felt powerful clawed hands reaching for him, grabbing him. Flailing his arms, he beat at the enemy he could not see. Following Hillary's lead, he stumbled back across the cavern floor toward the ledge that led upward to the gap through which they had entered.

"YEAAAGGGGGGHHHHHHHHHH!" Tony screamed from somewhere in the shadows.

Struggling to climb the rocky, sloping ledge, Brian witnessed Tony and Richard dragged toward a dark side passage by beings he couldn't see.

"We can't help them now!" Hillary yelled. "Keep going!"

They continued their ascent, sliding on the damp, slippery ledge. At the top Hillary clambered through the small opening, then helped to pull Brian up behind her.

"The limestone slabs!" he choked out between breaths. "Someone must have put them there to trap the invisible creatures in the cavern. The legend is true! The markings must be some kind of magical symbols that the monsters can't pass beyond. We've got to put the slabs back exactly like they were!"

Together they slid the heavy slabs into place, trying unsuccessfully to line up the odd markings. Then they raced along the upper passage toward the light.

Gasping in fear and pain, they burst through the cave opening and into the bright midday sunlight. Hillary fell sobbing to the ground.

Brian, lying next to her, gazed up at the bright sun, letting its warmth flood into him.

"We made it," Hillary murmured softly. "We're safe. We've got to go back for Tony and Richard. But first, we can go and get help."

Brian looked over to her and felt chilled to the bone.

"Maybe not," he whimpered, pointing to the ground. Although there was nothing to be seen around them, they were surrounded by a ring of shadows . . . shadows with huge bat wings and long-fingered hands with hooked claws. And the shadows were slowly closing in.

———>◆<———

A Dead Man's Chest

rowning, Mrs. Armstrong shuffled through a small stack of papers on her desk. "Ah, here it is," she said, standing and walking to the front of the class. "As you all know, it is considered quite an honor to be in the Wright's Cove Middle School Festival of the Pirates Pageant."

Glancing over at his best friend, Mike, Peter opened his mouth and put a finger on his tongue in a gagging gesture. Mike stifled a laugh.

"Those of you who tried out for the pageant, which is most of you, will be given a part," their teacher continued with a smile. "But now it is my pleasure to assign the lead roles, beginning with the evil old pirate captain himself, James Treager. Then we will all quickly review the script."

One by one she called out students' names and the characters they were to play.

Peter stopped listening and began to doodle pictures of pirates on his notebook. It wasn't that he didn't like the story. It was just that he had heard it so often. His mom worked at the maritime museum in town, and it was part of her job to publicize the nearly two-centuries-old tale that was the small town's claim to fame.

It seems that at one time in its history, Wright's Cove had been a place where a famous pirate, James Treager, took shelter from authorities. Known as "The Shark," the pirate had a reputation for being extremely brutal, and he and his crew terrorized the small village. They took food and supplies whenever they wanted and didn't hesitate to cruelly end the lives of anybody who got in the way.

Treager "stationed" men at the village at all times. When he returned from the sea and wished to come ashore, he would ring a bell on his ship. Unless he heard a similar bell rung by one of the pirates onshore signaling danger, he knew it was safe.

Nowadays the Festival of the Pirates was held annually in honor of the night the Shark was finally captured and executed. For an entire week, the townspeople would do their best to turn Wright's Cove back into the eighteenth-century seafarer's village it had once been. The event drew tourists from all over, so local businesspeople were always anxious to cooperate. On the final day everyone wore masks and costumes, and in a special pageant in the town square, students reenacted the capture itself.

According to historical record, Treager's reign of terror had come to an end when a brave young fisherman, Jeremiah Wright, rallied the townspeople to action. They captured the bell and all the pirate's men on land. When Treager's ship sailed into the harbor, there was no one to ring the warning bell. The unsuspecting pirates came ashore, where they were ambushed and finally captured. At midnight the bloodthirsty thugs were forced to pay for their crimes by leaping off the bluff that jutted out over the harbor. The sea-swept rocks below proved fatal to each of the villains, as well as to Treager himself.

Legend had it that before the Shark had been prodded off the edge, he turned his evil gaze on the townspeople and roared, "I will have my revenge! You have decided your own end. The sea cannot hold me or save you from your fate!"

But Jeremiah Wright stood boldly before the pirate and raised the brass bell that had lured him to his doom. "As long as this bell sounds to mark your death, Treager," he shouted above the howl of the wind, "you can never return to land. The sea will forever be your grave!" And with that, Treager was driven over the edge, his screams lost in the crashing of the waves on the rocks below.

Two hundred years later, few people actually believed the dramatic account of Treager's demise to be true, but the bell would always be rung at midnight at the height of the festivities.

"So are you crushed because you're not going to be in the pageant?" Mike asked sarcastically as he sat next to Peter in the lunchroom.

"I don't know if I can live through it," Peter shot back in a voice just as sarcastic and loud enough to be heard by two other friends, Adam and Kyle, who were walking up to join them.

"You *are* going to dress up, aren't you?" Kyle asked, sitting down.

"Sure," Peter answered. "That part's fun. I just wish they'd do something different once in a while. I mean, every year it's the same old thing."

Adam nodded in agreement. "Yeah, my dad says if Mayor Gates gives the same speech he always does before ringing the bell, he's going to start a campaign to throw him out of office."

Kyle laughed. "Nothing could get him to change that speech. He's been giving it for the past six years. I don't see why it's such a big deal anyway. Nobody really believes the story."

"What do you mean?" Peter said in surprise. "Of course it's true. There are stories about Treager and Wright's Cove in history books."

"Yeah, *that* part's true," Kyle admitted. "I meant the stuff about the bell and all. But I'll bet that after the pirates were snuffed, some smart guy just made up the rest of it because it sounded good and people would come to see the famous bell. You know what I think would happen if nobody rang it after the pageant?"

No one spoke.

"Exactly right," Kyle said with a smirk. "*Nothing.*"

"Except," offered Peter with a mischievous grin, "Mayor Gates would have a cow."

Mike grinned. "Now *that* is something I'd like to see."

"Me, too. I'll bet it would really freak a few people out," Peter mused. "You know, that gives me an idea." He motioned for his friends to come closer, then lowered his voice. "What if we make *sure* the bell doesn't ring by hiding it?"

"Right," Mike said with a smile. "How are we supposed to walk up in front of a few hundred people and swipe it? If you remember, it stays locked up at the museum until the pageant is over."

"That's right," Peter agreed, nodding. "But my mom has a set of keys to the museum, and I happen to know where she keeps them. She'd never notice if I borrowed them. Besides, we could get the bell and put the keys back before anyone knew they were missing."

Adam frowned. "How would we get the bell out of there without anybody seeing us, and what would we do with it?"

"Everybody will be at the pageant," Peter answered confidently. "And we have a whole week to figure out exactly what we're going to do with it. Let's start now."

• • • • • • • • • •

By the time the night of the pageant arrived, everyone in Wright's Cove was truly in the spirit of the festival, sporting striped T-shirts, colorful bandannas, and other pirate garb. In fact, Mr. Wojenski at the emporium had completely run out of black eye patches and plastic hand hooks.

With his mom's keys, it had been easy for Peter and his friends to get into the museum through the back entrance.

"See," Peter said triumphantly. "Just like I told you, everyone is at the pageant."

They had carefully worked out every step of the plan. Adam kept watch while Peter lifted the eight-inch-high brass bell from its display case. Holding the clapper to keep it silent, he placed their booty in a red-lined wooden chest where it was stored when not on display, and he snapped down the lock. The chest was about the size of a small suitcase, but it had metal handles on each side that made it easier to lift and carry.

"It's heavier than I thought it would be," Mike complained as he and Kyle each gripped a handle.

"It's all clear back here," Adam whispered. "Hurry!"

The four slipped out quickly and headed toward the beach. There was a small cave where the bluff slanted down to meet the sea. It was above the waterline at all times, and the entrance was easy to reach at low tide. Peter had checked the tide tables and decided that the cave would be the perfect hiding place for the bell.

"Hey," Mike called to Peter as they trudged across the sand on the darkened beach. "Let's stop for a minute. This thing is getting heavier."

Peter glanced at the glowing dial of his watch. It was twenty minutes to midnight. They had plenty of time to stash the bell and get back to town before anyone started searching.

"OK," he agreed, flopping down on the cool sand. Peter looked around and shivered. In the pale light of a half moon, the shoreline looked eerie and unreal. Turning slightly he could see the bright lights behind them. Sounds of the festivities drifted down the hill, but the town seemed miles away. Before him a slim line of foaming waves marked where the ocean met the shore, but beyond that there was . . . what? Peter felt a strange surge of fear. What if the story was really true. What if . . . he shook the thought away and glanced at the others. Everyone was quiet, obviously thinking the same thing.

After a few minutes Kyle whispered hesitantly, "Pete, you don't suppose . . . I mean . . . you don't *believe* that people can come back from the dead, do you?"

"No!" Peter answered firmly, but suddenly he was very aware of how alone they were on the desolate beach. "We'd better get this over with," he added, looking down at his watch. Then he caught his breath. It still read twenty minutes before midnight. He slapped the dial, but the numbers remained the same. "Oh no. I don't believe it. My watch is . . . " But he was silenced when Adam gasped and pointed toward the sea.

"Look!" Adam said, his voice filled with horror. "What are they?"

Several dark shapes seemed to be bobbing in the water about a hundred feet offshore. The boys stared in disbelief as more of the shapes came into view. They were people, or something like people, walking through the surf and heading toward the shore.

"Over there!" Kyle cried. "There's more!" Peter looked in the direction of Kyle's gaze. Five more dark figures were slogging steadily through the sea foam and onto the beach.

"And there!" Mike gestured wildly to the other side. "It's them, isn't it? We were wrong. The pirates *have* come back!"

"The bell!" Peter moaned. "We've got to ring the bell!" He dropped to his knees in the sand and fumbled with the chest. "It's locked!" he cried out. "It must have locked automatically when I snapped it shut. We've got to get it open!"

"Not me!" Kyle shouted. "I'm outta here!"

He started to run clumsily through the sand, and Adam

lurched after him. They hadn't gone but a few dozen yards when two wraithlike figures emerged from the shadows of the cliff. Their skin shimmered with a greenish glow, their eyes blazed red as blood, and the air grew thick and heavy with the foul smell of what they were—things too long under the sea. Reaching out with their long, taloned fingers, the phantoms gripped the two terrified boys, and dragged them back into the shadows.

"Kyle! Adam!" Mike screamed.

"It's too late!" Peter gasped. "We can't help them! We've got to try to get back to town and warn everyone." Wiping away tears with the back of his shaking hand, he tasted sand and salt . . . and fear. It was so overpowering that he could barely draw a breath, but he forced himself to move.

Grabbing one handle of the chest, he yelled to Mike to lift up the other side. "We can make it up the hill," he shouted. "We've got to get the bell back!"

Mike grabbed the other handle, and they began to struggle through the sand with the heavy chest. Peter stole a glance over his shoulder and saw that at least ten of the hideous specters were moving slowly up the beach.

"Keep going!" he screeched.

Slipping and sliding, the boys made it to the gravel path and started up. Every breath burned as Peter fought to keep his balance. They were almost halfway up when he felt his feet slide out from under him. Falling heavily, he cried out as the loose stone and pebbles of the path scraped across the bare flesh of his face. Then the handle of the chest slipped from his grasp.

With all the weight suddenly on him, Mike teetered at the edge of the path for a split second, and then with a wail of terror, toppled over and slid down the embankment. A shadowy figure below lunged toward him, and Mike's screams ceased.

Peter scrambled back to his feet. The bell was gone, but at least he could still warn the townspeople of the terrible doom that approached. Ignoring the sharp pain in his side, he began to run again. As the trail flattened out, the yelling and whooping of the townspeople grew louder. *They're still on the bluff*, he thought, turning in that direction. Suddenly he saw someone on the path ahead. Peter squinted, blinking away the dirt and tears. He recognized the gaudy pirate costume and familiar mask. It was Mayor Gates. With a last burst of effort he raced toward him.

"Mayor Gates!" Peter gasped. "The pirates . . . it's all true! They've come back, just like Treager said they would. We've got to warn everyone while there's still time . . . before they get here."

Peter stopped. Mayor Gates was laughing. "I'm not joking, Mayor!" Peter shouted, his fear mixing with anger and frustration. "It's all true, and soon they'll be here!"

Slowly the tall man gripped his mask and lowered it inch by inch. "You are wrong, lad," he hissed evilly. "We're *already* here."

In horror, Peter realized that the cries coming from the bluff were shrieks of terror. And he was gazing into the cold, soulless eyes of James Treager himself.

"Come along, my boy," the phantom commanded, clenching Peter in his icy grip. "It is time for the final act."

The Hole
in the Ceiling

ichael knew that his two-year-old sister Emily was a remarkable child. His best friend, Bill, also had a sister Emily's age, but the two girls were like night and day. Jeannie, Bill's sister, was a total pain. She was always getting into Bill's stuff, and she didn't make much sense when she tried to talk.

Emily, on the other hand, was well behaved. She already spoke fairly well and could even hold a simple conversation. But Emily had a wild imagination, and sometimes the things she said were a little odd.

One day while Michael was doing his homework, she toddled into the room and asked, "What are you doing?"

Michael looked up from his math book to see Emily standing right next to him, her eyes filled with curiosity.

"Homework," he said with a groan.

"I will help you," Emily offered, completely serious.

Michael shook his head. "I don't think so," he replied. "Not unless you can multiply fractions."

"Pop-pops can," Emily said. "He knows lots of things."

"Right." Michael watched as she went to his window, placed her tiny hands against the glass, and peered out.

"But he only comes when it is dark. Not dark like this," she explained. "Dark like at night."

Michael glanced out the window. The afternoon was dull and dreary. According to the morning weather report, a major storm was barreling across the Pacific toward the coast. It was supposed to hit early that evening.

"Pop-pops is the one with the wings, isn't it?" he asked. Emily had so many imaginary friends it was hard to keep track of them, but this was one she had made up a few days ago. "He lives in the attic and comes in to play through a hole in the ceiling, right?"

"No," she said giggling. "He doesn't live in the *attic*. He lives in the *ceiling*. I can see him and hear him sometimes, but he can't come in until he finds a way to open the door." She looked at her brother with a smile. "Would you tell me a story?" she asked, abruptly changing the subject.

Michael glanced at his math book. "Not now, Em." He sighed. "I've got to get this done. Why don't you go play with your dolls or something?"

Emily scowled slightly. "They won't play with me today. Pop-pops scared them 'cause he looks icky. He scared them when he made them fly. He said I could fly, too, if I wanted and so could my toys. He said he will teach me everything he knows." She paused, seeing that she'd lost Michael's attention. "I will ask Mommy if I can watch a video. 'Bye, Michael."

She closed the door and Michael smiled as he heard his precocious little sister running down the hall.

By dinnertime the storm had begun. Outside, the trees twisted and bowed in the wind, and a cold rain fell in ragged sheets.

"We're in for a big one," Michael's father commented as the family gathered at the table. "On my way home, traffic was backed up all the way up to the interstate." He shook his head. "I'm sure glad I don't have to be out on a night like this. I don't think we've had anything this bad since the night Emily was born. Remember?"

"How could I forget?" Michael's mother responded with a laugh. "Half the county was evacuated because of a flood warning, and I was in the delivery room."

A bolt of lightning flashed brightly outside the dining room window. Michael counted to himself: *one thousand one, one thousand two, one thousand three* . . . then a deep roll of thunder rumbled overhead.

"Then what happened, Mom?" Michael asked politely. He'd heard the story before, but he knew she liked to tell it.

"Well, everyone at the hospital was doing their best, but with the storm and all, there were a lot of emergencies. All the nurses had their hands full. Then just as Emmie was being born, the electricity went completely off." She snapped her fingers. "Just like that! Of course, the emergency lights kicked in right away, but you can imagine what it was like."

Michael's dad shot Emily a grin. "But my little girl made it safely into the world."

"That she did," Michael's mom went on, smiling at his sister. "But it was quite an experience. The lights went off a few times, if I remember."

"Uh-huh," Emily chimed in. "That was when the blue lady put me with you and took the other one."

Everyone turned to look at Emily. She was at it again. Every time Michael's mom told the story of Emily's birth, the two-year-old mentioned that blue lady.

"Let me tell the story, honey," her mom said. "I know you want to join in the conversation, but you couldn't possibly remember that night."

"Yes, I can," the little girl answered simply.

Michael's parents exchanged glances.

"Well," her mom said softly, thinking back to that night. "Actually, I did imagine that there was another woman in my hospital room, but I certainly don't think she was blue. Anyway, I was pretty tired and I fell asleep for a bit, but I do remember waking up for a moment or two and noticing this woman huddled in the corner. The room was dark and I couldn't see very well, but she seemed very upset. I asked the nurse about it later. She said that no one else had been there and I must have been dreaming." Michael's mom shrugged. "Still . . . I do remember . . . "

"Now don't you start imagining things," his dad interrupted. "We already have one expert in make-believe in the family." He smiled, looking at his daughter. "Our own little Emily."

Emily furrowed her brow. "What's an X-perk?" she asked, and everyone laughed.

• • • • • • • • • • •

"Aaaaaaaaaa-choo!" Michael parked his bike in the garage, pulled a tissue from his pocket, and dabbed at his nose. He'd always had problems with his allergies in the spring, but this season was particularly bad.

"I'm home, Mom!" he called out, slamming the door behind him. He knew that she had made a doctor's appointment for him that afternoon, so he'd come straight home from school.

"Hi, sweetie," his mom greeted him, car keys in hand. "We've got to get going right away."

"But I thought my appointment was at four," Michael said, looking at his watch.

"It is," she responded, helping Emily with her raincoat. "But I noticed Emily has a funny rash on her arms. Dr. Tokado said he could take a look at her, too, if we came in right away."

"Look," Emily said proudly as she pushed up her sleeves. Michael could see that she had a scaly bluish streak of dry skin on the inside of each arm.

"Yuck!" He made a face. "It's the creeping crud!"

But the doctor didn't call it that. In fact, he had no name for Emily's strange rash. He gave Michael's mom some ointment to put on it and said to watch it for a few days. If it didn't go away or if it got worse, he wanted to see Emily again.

Later that night after putting Emily to bed, Michael's parents went to a neighborhood watch meeting, leaving Michael in charge. He was stretched out on his bed doing his homework when he suddenly heard his sister giggling in her room down the hall. It sounded like she was having a ball in there. He glanced at the clock in irritation.

"She should be asleep by now," he muttered. Closing his notebook, he marched down the hall and opened the door to his sister's room. "You're supposed to be . . ." he started to scold her, but the words caught in his throat.

Emily was sitting up and holding her hands outward, moving her fingers slightly in a circular motion. In the dim glow from the night light near her bed, he could see that her eyes were gleaming a very dull red.

"Look, Mikey!" she squealed happily. "I can do it, just like Pop-pops said!"

Turning to see where Emily was pointing, Michael gasped. Several of Emily's toys were suspended in air, moving in a lazy circle as if under the grip of some strange force. A sudden flash of lightning lit up the fantastic scene, and Michael choked back a scream.

"I can do it real good!" she added with satisfaction. "Watch!" Her eyes glowed a brighter crimson and the toys began to orbit around the room faster and faster.

"Stop it!" Michael yelled. "What are you doing?"

The toys suddenly dropped to the floor, and Emily began to cry. "You scared me!" she sobbed.

Michael backed slowly out of the room and raced to the phone to call the neighbor's house where his parents were. But when his dad got on the phone, he knew he'd never be able to explain what he'd seen. "Just get home," he told his father. "And *hurry*!"

• • • • • • • • • • •

"Wait a minute, Mike," his dad said, trying to calm him down after he'd heard the whole story. "That's crazy. You must have made a mistake."

"No, Dad!" Michael shouted. "Thinking you see something in the corner that isn't there . . . *that's* a mistake. This was a bunch of toys flying through the air right past my head. I'm not making it up! I know what I saw!"

"She's asleep," his mom announced as she entered the living room. "Her room looks just the same as when we left it, Michael. Now, honey . . ." She walked over to him and gently combed back his hair with her fingers. "I hear what you're saying, but there must be some other explanation."

Michael pulled away from his mother in frustration.

"Look, it's late," his dad said firmly. "We'll talk about this tomorrow."

"Fine," Michael said. Angry at not being believed, he stomped upstairs to his room.

Later that night a crash of thunder woke Michael from a dead sleep. Blinking, he saw a small pale figure beside his bed.

"Emily!" he nearly shouted, sitting up with a start.

"Mikey," his sister said, close to tears. "They said I have to go with them. Will you go, too?"

Michael rubbed his eyes. "What are you talking about?"

"They found a place to come through," she said earnestly. "I know *I* have to go. But I want *you* to go with me. I will miss you too much if you don't."

Michael looked into the sweet face of his little sister. In the past he might have told her she was dreaming and sent her back to bed, but after what he had seen that night, he didn't know what to think.

"Come on," he said soothingly. "I'll stay in your room with you tonight. *They* aren't going to take you anywhere."

Grabbing a pillow and blanket, Michael followed Emily down the hall and stretched out on the floor beside her small bed. Soon he could hear the slow, even breathing that meant she had fallen asleep. But he wasn't so lucky. The storm grew even more intense and the trees outside the window cast strange shadows on the ceiling. Michael watched them shifting, then all at once realized that there was something else on the ceiling—or rather *in* it.

From where he lay, Michael made out what looked like a small dark hole in the ceiling. To his amazement it was growing wider and wider right before his eyes! Feeling his heart start to pound, he then saw two figures slipping through the opening and into the room. Silhouetted for a moment against the window, the two figures moved toward his sister's bed.

Gripped by terror, Michael felt as if he were made of stone. He *had* to do something. The figures were reaching for Emily!

"Nooooooooo!" he screamed, finally leaping to his feet. But as he did, one of the beings whirled toward him and tossed him away as easily as a discarded shoe.

Suddenly the door to Emily's room flew open and the overhead light snapped on, flooding the place with light. Michael took in the scene along with his startled parents, who were now at the door. Two creatures, tall with scaly, pale blue skin and leathery wings tucked down at their shoulders, were standing there. One had Emily in its arms, while the other raised its hand and released a surge of something that looked like lightning. For a moment both creatures' eyes glowed a dim red. "You will remain where you are," one of them ordered in a tinny voice. Oddly enough, Michael felt that he had *sensed* the command rather than heard it. He wanted to call out to his parents, to run to them, but as hard as he tried he could not budge. By their inaction, he knew that his parents must be somehow paralyzed as well.

The creature continued. "We do not want to harm you in any way," it said. "We have come from a world and time far in the future to correct a terrible mistake."

Michael and his parents watched in disbelief, still unable to move, as the creature spoke again. "We do not expect you to understand, but somehow, for a short time two of your years ago, an unpredicted tear opened in the thin veil of space-time that separates our world from yours."

As the being "spoke," Michael noticed that two other figures entered through the dark opening in the ceiling. They appeared to be two females, one an adult covered with the same pale blue scales as the other creatures. The other was a child who looked much like Emily.

"This woman from our world and her newborn child slipped through the rift and became lost for only a few moments," the creature explained. "We managed to pull them back before the tear sealed, or so we thought. But as the child grew, and we attempted to instruct her in the use of her power, she could not seem to learn. Our mistake became clear to us. We had recovered an Earth infant instead of our own child. This child who you believed to be your daughter is ours," the being said, tenderly stroking Emily's hair. Now she didn't seem to be afraid.

"We have tried for quite a while to return your Earth child and take back our own, and now we have succeeded in bridging the gap that separates our worlds. But we must hurry. We have only a short time to correct our mistake."

Michael looked at Emily as she ran happily into the arms of the alien woman approaching her.

"No!" Michael heard his mother struggling to cry out the words. "She's our baby. You can't take her!"

"We have no choice," the creature answered, as he gently nudged forward the other frightened child, who *did* look entirely human. "I know you must love her, but she can no longer stay with you. As infants, our two life forms seem to look much alike, but as Emily grows she will become as we are. You would have soon learned the truth if we had not come to make the exchange." He reached out and turned Emily's small arm to the light. The dried skin Michael had seen earlier was now a distinct covering of pale blue scales. "You see, the change has already begun. She will have no place here soon, and if not directed properly, the powers she possesses could be very dangerous."

Emily turned to her new family and smiled. "I want to go," she said simply. "I want to be with Pop-pops."

And with that, one of the creatures gripped her small hand, guided her toward the opening, and lifted her through.

Before the last creature slipped away, it glanced at Michael and his parents almost kindly, raised its hand, and shone a pale blue beam into their eyes. "Do not worry. In moments none of you will remember this has ever taken place. It will be easier that way." Then it departed and the hole closed behind it.

Michael felt the paralysis that held him suddenly release. He looked over at his parents, who seemed to be almost in a trance. Then his dad smiled as his mother sat on the edge of the bed and took her new daughter in her arms.

"Don't be frightened, Emmie," she soothed, obviously not remembering that this wasn't Emily. "It's only a storm. Mommy and Daddy are here."

Michael took a step toward his family . . . then stopped. His new baby sister was looking over his mom's shoulder at a doll across the room. Her eyes began to glow red and she reached out her hand. Michael gasped as the doll flew through the air to her chubby outstretched hand.

"Mom, Dad!" he cried out. "Those creatures . . . they were wrong. She did learn. She has the power!"

"What are you talking about, Mike?" his father asked. "Stop it. You'll frighten your sister."

Michael looked deep into the little girl's glowing eyes and felt a deep sense of dread.

"I . . . I . . ." he started, then stopped. He couldn't recall what it was he had wanted to say. It had seemed important, but now he just couldn't remember.

The Family Honor

ideon Mitchell couldn't believe what he was hearing. "We're going to England?" he asked his mother again. "Do you really mean it?"

"I sure do," she answered with a big smile. "We leave next Saturday."

"This is great!" Gideon responded, his smile revealing his enthusiasm.

"Your dad and I know how hard it's been on you this summer with both of us working so much," she said. "I hope this makes up for it." Gideon grinned from ear to ear, showing that it did. True, his summer had started out pretty bland, with no hope for any kind of family vacation, but luckily his dad's promise of turning a business trip into a family excursion had now been realized.

"We're going to England!" Gideon cried. "Of course that makes up for it."

"Now keep in mind that your father may have to work most of the time we're there," his mom reminded him. "But I've managed to clear my schedule for a week so you and I can spend as much time as we like together. Maybe you'll even help me pick out a few new pieces," she added. "I'm sure they have some great things over there."

"Sure, Mom," Gideon said happily. "It'd be fun."

Gideon's mom was an interior decorator, and she was always searching for unusual antiques for her clients. In spite of her invitation to join her in the hunt, Gideon realized it was likely that he wouldn't see too much of either of his parents on this trip. As usual, they would get involved in their work, leaving him to entertain himself. But he didn't mind. He would be in England, the land of King Arthur and the Knights of the Round Table. *And* the land of his ancestors.

For as long as he could remember, Gideon had felt that England was his true home, and his greatest wish was to have been a brave knight, riding out on some dangerous quest. Perhaps that was partly because in real life he was rather fearful and chose to avoid anything that might be even slightly hazardous.

But this time, while Mom and Dad are working, I'm going to strike out on my own! Gideon thought.

The next day Gideon told his next-door neighbor, Cody, all about the trip his parents were taking him on. "England is where the Rolling Stones and the Beatles are from!" Cody exclaimed. "My dad has all the records those guys ever made. And cool new groups are always starting up there. Maybe your folks will even take you to a concert."

"I don't think so," Gideon said, laughing. "Besides, we're going to stay with my dad's cousins. They live in a little village out in the country, called Ravenshire. I don't think they have any concerts out there."

"Bummer," Cody responded sympathetically.

Gideon shook his head. "I don't mind. What I really want to see is the castle where one of my ancestors used to live."

"Get outta here!" Cody said raising an eyebrow. "Are you trying to tell me that you're related to the King of England or something?"

"No, nothing like that," Gideon responded seriously. "Lots of people lived in castles there hundreds of years ago. And it so happens that one of my ancestors on my dad's side was a real knight."

"With armor and everything?" Cody asked, his eyes wide.

Gideon nodded proudly. "Yup. His name was Sir Linovore, and the castle was actually his home."

Cody looked at Gideon in awe. "That's wild. Are you going to get to sleep in the castle?"

Gideon shook his head. "No, nobody can stay there anymore. It's like a tourist place now. But my great-uncle is the caretaker, and he's going to let me go with him every day when he goes to work, so I can do anything I want there," he lied. Actually, it was just half a lie. His great-uncle really was the caretaker, but Gideon had never met him, so he didn't know if he would be allowed to explore the castle freely or not.

"That's so cool. You know, a lot of old castles are supposed to be haunted," Cody said. "Maybe your family's is too."

"Well, there *is* supposed to be a ghost," Gideon answered, remembering the story his dad had told him. "Sir Linovore had two sons, and one of them was supposed to be guarding the gate when the castle was under attack or something. Instead he ran away, and nobody ever found out what happened to him. His younger brother took his place at the gate, but he got killed. So the legend is that Sir Linovore's younger son haunts the castle."

"Wow," Cody declared in admiration. "Your own family ghost. Maybe if you're lucky you'll get to see him."

"Yeah," Gideon agreed, trying to ignore the sudden, tiny stab of fear that inexplicably gnawed at his belly. "If I'm lucky."

• • • • • • • • • • •

The rest of the week passed so slowly that Gideon thought Saturday would never arrive. Finally the big day came, and he found himself strapped securely into the seat of a big 747 transatlantic passenger jet bound for England. Once the plane was in the air, he pulled out the two new books his dad had bought him. One was a collection of legends about brave knights in shining armor, but the other was the one he really loved.

It was a slender volume with a leatherlike cover of dark moss green. In the center, his family name, Mitchell, was embossed in rich, gold-leaf letters. Gideon ran his hand over the cover, then opened the book to the center. There, on heavy, cream-colored paper, was a drawing of an elaborate tree. A network of horizontal lines started down at the trunk and continued up into the leafy crown. It was a small family tree, and with his parents' help Gideon had already been able to fill in the names of family members as far back as his great-great-grandparents.

He laid the book on his lap and gazed out the window, watching the eastern coastline of the United States fall behind. Slowly Gideon's eyelids began to droop. *Soon I'll be able to fill in the rest of the blanks,* he thought, patting the book and then drifting off to sleep. When he awoke, Gideon and his parents had touched down on English soil.

Heathrow Airport was so noisy and crowded with travelers that Gideon's parents almost didn't spot his dad's older cousin, Christopher. He rushed up to greet them after they had gone through the customs line, where their passports were checked and stamped.

"You'll want some food and rest after your long journey," Christopher said pleasantly as he stowed their luggage in the back of his van. "Stephanie has a fine shepherd's pie waiting for us at home, and she has your rooms all ready." He looked at Gideon. "And don't you worry, my boy; tomorrow your great-uncle Albert will be giving you all a VIP tour of Ravenshire Castle. Your dad here told me you've a great interest in your English ancestry."

Gideon nodded groggily, and his dad threw an arm around his shoulder. "He'll be breaking down the door at Ravenshire Castle," Gideon's dad said with a hearty laugh, "as soon as his jet lag wears off."

•••••••••••

True to his father's prediction, the following morning Gideon could barely control his excitement as they walked over the mile-long, rutted dirt road that led from Ravenshire village to the castle itself.

"There she is," Christopher pointed as they rounded a grass-covered hill. At first Gideon stared in wonder at the large stone structure that squatted like a hulking beast in the valley below. But as they drew closer, he experienced a rising surge of uneasiness. Ever since he could remember he had wanted to visit Ravenshire Castle, but now he struggled with the urge to flee.

Why am I such a chicken? he asked himself, fighting the feeling that remained with him even when his great-uncle Albert met them at the wide stone entry. The same unsettling sense of foreboding stayed with him as Albert guided the family through the dim, drafty corridors.

With a flourish, Albert threw open a heavy wooden door to a large room in the back of the castle. "And this is the armory," he announced with an air of authority. Gideon looked in wonder at about a dozen suits of armor standing against one wall. On the opposite side was a display of medieval weapons.

"Boy," his father said as he studied a metal ball covered with long, sharp spikes. It was attached to a wooden handle by a short chain. "I guess this could have done some real damage."

"Yes, indeed," Albert answered. "One sound whack from this evil thing could cave in any poor devil's head. It's called a mace."

In a glass case beside a fairly small suit of armor, Gideon noticed some sort of coat made with tiny links of chain. "Is this a hauberk?" he asked his great-uncle.

Albert's face lit up. "Why, yes, young sir! It seems you know your armor quite well." He opened the case and lifted out the metal garment. "It was worn over a leather tunic and under a breastplate. Here, feel how heavy it is." He handed the weighty clothing over to Gideon.

Gideon reached out and took the hauberk. It felt oddly familiar. "Wow, it must weigh thirty pounds!"

"That's about right," the old man said nodding. "It was strong enough to turn the blow of a sword or a lance, but not strong enough to save the poor unfortunate lad who wore it last."

"What do you mean?" Gideon asked.

Albert pointed to a ragged opening on one side. "That was worn by Cecil, Sir Linovore's youngest son, on the night that he died. He was mortally wounded by the sword that made that very breach."

Gideon touched the opening with his finger. "Ow!" he yelped, suddenly feeling a terrible pain in his own side. He quickly dropped the garment.

Albert and his parents stared at him, startled.

"I'm sorry," Gideon said sheepishly. "I don't know why I . . . I . . . "

"No harm done," his great-uncle said, picking up the hauberk and gently putting it back in its case.

• • • • • • • • • •

The next morning Gideon's parents drove into London, but Gideon begged to stay so that he could visit the castle once again. Uncle Albert was quite pleased to have an eager audience and was willing to explain anything Gideon wanted to know.

"What happened the night that Cecil died?" he asked as his great-uncle guided him down the wide main hall with its worn but richly woven tapestries. The old man didn't answer until they entered the family portrait gallery. He led Gideon to a huge oil painting of a boy about thirteen years old. An ornate brass plaque underneath identified him as Cecil.

"There had been a long-standing feud between the lord of this castle and another lord," Albert began. "Sir Linovore's enemies had raided the outlying lands several times, but one night they attacked the castle itself with great force. Linovore's older son had been told to remain at the wall above the main gate to warn of any danger, but when the attack began, he left his post." As he spoke, Albert's tone was sad, as if the events had just taken place yesterday rather than centuries before. "The attack was repelled, but not before young Cecil had taken his brother's place and died in his stead. Some superstitious people claim that the young master's ghost still roams the castle, waiting for his brother to return."

"What was the older brother's name?" Gideon asked. "And what happened to him?" Although he didn't understand why, he was almost afraid to hear the answer.

"No one knows what happened to him," Albert said, shrugging his shoulders. "Some say his disappearance was the work of Glyvn, the court sorcerer, but no one wanted to ask because they feared the power of the old man's magic." Albert paused as if thinking about what he had just said,

100

and then went on. "After Cecil was buried, every reference to his brother was stricken from any records. No one was allowed to say his name. In fact, anything that belonged to the older boy or would remind his family of him was burned." Albert motioned to a large blank space on the stone wall where another portrait should have hung.

Glancing back at the painting of Cecil, Gideon suddenly felt a twinge of icy terror ripple down his spine. He could see the face of another young boy reflected in the glass over the canvas.

He whirled around just in time to see a figure retreating from the entryway to the chamber. "Who was that?" he asked his great-uncle. "There was someone standing in the . . . " But Gideon stopped in midsentence. His uncle was no longer there, and the dim, cold room had changed. Now a warm fire roared in the huge stone fireplace, and dozens of lit candles flickered from metal sconces on the walls.

"What's going on?" Gideon whispered aloud. Then something else caught his eye. The large blank space on the wall was no longer empty. A huge portrait hung there. Its colors were vibrant and new, as if it had recently been painted. He closed his eyes tightly, willing himself not to look, but he couldn't resist. Slowly he turned his gaze upward to peer at the face of the boy in the portrait. It was his own!

Horrified, Gideon gasped and ran from the room into the main hall. "Uncle Albert!" he yelled. "Where are you?" But his cry merely echoed off the stone walls, which were awash with the light of flickering candles. Aghast, Gideon noticed that the tapestries that had only moments ago seemed aged and worn now appeared perfectly new and exquisite in fresh hues of bright scarlet and royal blue. A crimson carpet covered the cold stone floor at his feet, but it was what he saw on the hall staircase where the carpet ended that made his heart leap. It was a young boy . . . Cecil . . . who was slowly descending.

"No!" Gideon shouted. "You're dead! Stay away from me!" Turning on his heels, Gideon raced back into the gallery. There Albert stared at him in surprise.

"What on earth has gotten into you, my boy?" the old man asked with a worried expression.

In panic, Gideon looked from the cold, dark fireplace, to the empty candle sconces, to the bare space on the gallery wall.

"I thought . . . " Gideon began, then stopped. "I don't know, Uncle Albert. I guess I just let my imagination run away with me."

• • • • • • • • • • •

That night Gideon tossed restlessly in bed. In his dreams he heard the sounds of battle raging all around him—the clanging of swords against armor, the shouts of soldiers, the pounding of horses' hooves on hard, cold ground. He began to run, slowly at first, then faster and faster, but he kept returning to the same place; a stone rampart overlooking the gate of Ravenshire Castle. And it was cold, so very cold.

All at once Gideon's eyes snapped open and he looked around in bewilderment. He was standing just inside the massive entry hall of the castle. "How in the world did I get here?" he cried, then rushed to the heavy wooden door. It was securely locked. For a moment he pounded on the ancient oak. But it was useless.

"Get a grip here," he told himself, trying to calm his racing pulse. "I was probably just sleepwalking. So if I got myself in here, I can get myself out." He took a tentative step toward the main hall. From somewhere outside came the plaintive wail of a dog, sending a tremor through Gideon's entire body. He tried to peer into the shadows that loomed all around him. Then he noticed a slight glow coming from a chamber near the central staircase. *That's the library*, he thought. *Maybe Uncle Albert is here.* Hesitantly, step by step, he worked his way along the darkened corridor until he stood directly in front of the library's door. Slowly he turned the knob and the door swung open, its hinges squealing in protest.

Gideon eased into the book-lined room and saw that the glow was coming from behind another door, one he hadn't noticed when his uncle had first shown him the library. Now that door was slightly ajar. Steeling himself, Gideon swallowed his fear and slipped through the opening into a different room.

Dominated by a huge desk covered with parchment scrolls and jars of colored liquids and powders, the small room smelled of exotic incense mingled with wax and smoke. A very old man sat at the desk scratching something onto parchment with a feather quill. He looked up at Gideon, and the boy recoiled in horror. The old man's eyes seemed like dark, fathomless pools that allowed him to see all of Gideon's thoughts.

"I was waiting for you." The man's deep voice echoed in the stillness. "I told you that you could not avoid your fate, no matter how far in time you travel. Ravenshire will always call you back." He rose deliberately and painfully from his chair and hobbled toward Gideon. "Now it is time to return things to the way they should be."

"No!" Gideon screamed. He twisted around and darted from the little room, through the library, and into the main hall, where he halted with a jolt. There on the stairs stood a shimmering specter of a teenage boy.

"You have finally come, dear brother," the thing moaned, starting to float toward him down the gloomy corridor.

Gideon let out a tortured scream and ran without thought of where he was going. All at once he heard his mother's voice calling him from somewhere in the castle.

"Gideon! Where are you?"

"Mom!" Gideon shrieked, racing to the main entrance.

Now he heard his great-uncle Albert trying to soothe her. "Now, Claire, I told you he wouldn't be in the castle. I locked the door when I left. There was no way he could have gotten in."

Gideon called to his mother again, but she was already allowing his great-uncle to guide her back outside. "He probably sneaked out to do a little exploring," Albert was saying. "You know how adventurous boys can be. When we get back to the cottage we'll find him sitting up having a cup of hot chocolate with Stephanie and Christopher. Just you wait and see."

"Don't leave, Mom!" Gideon cried. "I am here!"

"They cannot hear you," a deep voice said gently. "You are no longer of their time."

Gideon turned to see the old man he had encountered earlier. "You are of his time now," the aged fellow said, pointing out into the courtyard where a young boy in medieval garb was slipping a bridle onto a large, muscular horse, the kind that knights of old rode into battle centuries ago.

Gideon faced the man, who he now knew was the court sorcerer Albert had told him about. "Is there nothing you can do for me, Glyvn?" Gideon asked. He could sense the armed warriors approaching stealthily through the shadowy hills beyond the castle gates.

"I have done too much already by trying to send you forward in time where you were reborn," the aged man answered. "But now I know that there is no place on earth, in this time or any other, where you can hide. You must face your responsibility—one you shirked long ago." The sorcerer raised his hand. "Go, Gideon. It is time to stop your brother, Cecil, from doing the task and suffering the fate meant for you."

Gideon nodded. From a distant place in time and space he could hear his mother calling him, but his place was on the castle rampart. It was time to set things right, and he knew it. Turning slowly, Gideon walked toward the winding stairs without looking back.

❖

A Face in the Crowd

elly sat up and looked toward the surf. The midday sunlight splashed across the waves and splintered into hundreds of dancing beams. Kelly shielded her eyes and searched the shoreline for her family. Finally she spotted her parents and younger sister building a sand castle. Kelly smiled. Her five-year-old sister, Megan, was busy "decorating" the castle with bits of ruffly, dark green seaweed.

Closing her book, Kelly glanced around. It was only the first weekend of June. There was still a whole week of school left, but the beach was already crowded. People were relaxing, playing volleyball, wading, and jogging along the shoreline. Swimmers were bobbing up and down in the plunging waves, laughing and shouting.

Kelly leaned back again, took a deep breath of the salty air, and closed her eyes as she listened to the pleasant sounds. Suddenly the shouts of joy and playfulness turned to awful shrieks mingled with dozens of urgent voices. Startled, Kelly looked up. She saw the lifeguard race toward the ocean and dive into the churning waves. All at once it seemed that everyone was up and moving. Kelly jumped to her feet and looked to where her parents and sister had been playing. The sand castle was there, being trampled by the gathering crowd, but she couldn't see her family anywhere. Frantically she scanned the shoreline.

"Mom! Dad!" she cried out, joining the rush of people.

As she was pushed and jostled by the sea of onlookers, Kelly could feel her heart pounding louder than the crashing waves. Where were her parents? Where was Megan?

"Look!" a nearby woman gasped. "The lifeguard has someone. Can you see who it is?"

"Oh, no!" Kelly cried as she tried to force her way through the throng. *Please, please don't let it be any of my family*, she pleaded silently.

Suddenly Kelly felt someone touch her shoulder, and she heard a familiar voice say her name. With a flood of relief she turned to see her mother.

"We were so worried about you," Kelly's mom said, slipping her arm around her waist.

"I was worried about you, too!" Kelly returned sincerely. She looked around. "Where're Dad and Megan?"

"They're over there," her mom said, pointing toward the edge of the crowd. "Come on. I don't want to lose you again."

As they joined the others, the crowd appeared to draw back, and Kelly saw the lifeguard struggling to pull a heavyset man onto the beach. The man was pale and limp.

Another lifeguard sprinted to help. "Please, give them room!" he commanded.

Without a word, Kelly leaned against her mother. The noisy crowd became silent as the young man and woman worked determinedly to start the ashen-faced victim breathing again. But he remained still, his eyes staring vacantly toward the sky.

"What's going to happen, Dad?" Kelly asked with concern, hearing a siren wailing in the distance.

Her father shook his head and lifted Megan into his arms. "I don't think he's going to make it," he said somberly. "We should go," he added.

Kelly shivered, feeling suddenly chilled. And though there wasn't a cloud in the sky, the bright, sunny day now seemed pale and drab. Seagulls circled overhead, their calls resembling mournful cries. She turned to look out at the empty ocean, and then quickly caught her breath. A tall, dark-haired woman was standing ankle-deep in the water, staring coldly at the man who had drowned. She was wearing a gray long-sleeved dress with a high, old-fashioned collar. The hem of her full-length skirt swirled in the foaming surf.

The woman seemed oddly familiar to Kelly. It was more than just the outfit that she somehow recognized, it was something about the lack of emotion . . . the indifference in her expression—Kelly had seen that woman somewhere before.

"Mom," Kelly said touching her mother's arm. "Look at that woman. Where do we know her from? Don't you think it's weird for someone to wear a dress like that to the beach?"

Her mom looked in the direction that Kelly was staring. "What woman, honey? I don't see who you mean."

Kelly turned to look at her mother. "The one in the long dress," she said pointing. "She's standing in . . ." Kelly stopped and let her hand drop. "That's funny. She's gone."

Her mother shrugged. "She probably just got lost in the crowd like you did."

Just then an emergency vehicle ground to a halt on the sand, its siren still blaring. "Come on," Kelly's mom urged soberly. "Let's go and give the paramedics room to do their job."

At dinner that night, Kelly didn't feel like eating, and her parents understood. Later she stretched out on her bed in her darkened room, staring out at the starry night sky. She absentmindedly ran one finger across the trunk of her small, well-worn stuffed elephant, Peanuts.

"It's just so sad," Kelly whispered sleepily to the little animal. "I wonder if that poor man had a family." She felt the slight sting of tears as she wearily closed her eyes and fell asleep. Drifting in a dream world, she could still see the man's sightless stare. At first the image was very distinct, then slowly his features began to change. They rearranged themselves into another pale image. All at once Kelly found herself gazing at the strange woman in gray whom she had seen at the beach that day. The image in her mind burned itself into the space in front of her until it seemed as if the woman were staring in through the slightly open window of the second-floor bedroom, her haggard eyes hidden in shadow. Kelly tried to scream, but no sound would leave her throat. She tried to move, but nothing happened. It was as if every muscle in her body had turned to stone.

Then, as impossible as it seemed, the gaunt woman floated through the darkness, closer and closer toward the window. Her long gleaming hair fluttered in the night breeze.

No! Kelly shrieked in her mind, helpless as the woman slowly raised her hand in a gesture of command, and the window slid open even farther. *No, Get away! GET AWAY!*

Kelly sat straight up in bed, her hands aching. She had gripped the sheets so tightly that the blood had drained from her fingertips. She gaped into the shadows of her room. Peanuts had tumbled to the floor beside the bed. The window was as it had been, slightly open, and there was no phantom woman staring in at her.

"I must have been dreaming," Kelly sighed aloud. She gathered up Peanuts and slipped under the covers. She still had the creepy feeling that she had seen the spectral woman before. *Perhaps in another nightmare*, she thought. With one last look at the window, Kelly soon fell asleep.

• • • • • • • • • • •

"I can't wait!" Wendy exclaimed, as she and Kelly walked to school the next morning. Kelly and Wendy had become best friends since Wendy and her family had moved next door five months earlier. "We're all going to have such a great time this summer. Maureen said that we're going to be able to go horseback riding at the Givens Ranch. She knows, because her mom took her there to actually see the camp to decide if she liked it. *And* there's a new camp swimming pool . . . Olympic size! Wait until Nora hears about that. She'll just die. But I guess Maureen's probably already told her all about it. What do you think?" Wendy paused for a breath. "Well?" she said expectantly.

Kelly said nothing.

Wendy stopped and put her hands on her hips. "Earth to Kelly. Are you even listening to me?"

"Oh, I'm sorry." Kelly smiled sheepishly. "I was thinking about something else. What were you saying?"

Wendy shook her head and started walking again. "It wasn't important. We'll be leaving for camp this weekend. We'll have plenty of time to talk about it on the train, and Maureen can tell you about it herself. C'mon, let's cut through the park." Wendy took Kelly's arm and gave her a concerned look. "Are you still thinking about that guy on the beach? I guess it must have been pretty awful to see someone die."

Kelly stopped abruptly. She gazed out at the soccer field, and memories . . . very unpleasant memories . . . began to crowd in. "I saw it happen once before," she said softly. "A year ago."

In her mind she could recall the last time she had seen a fatal accident, and it was right here on this very corner. It had been a terrible experience, and Kelly had always tried not to think about it. But now it was all so clear in her mind—as if it were happening all over again right in front of her eyes.

The park had been filled with people. She and her friends were practicing some soccer moves. Old Mr. Levy had watched them for a while, then walked away. He must not have been paying attention to the traffic light when he stepped into the street. Kelly hadn't actually seen the accident, but she'd heard the squeal of the tires and the loud, sickening thud.

And now there was something else tugging at her thoughts. Kelly glanced at the low rise behind the picnic area of the park and the terrible memory came flooding back. That was where she had first seen her. The woman in gray—she had been there on that awful day a year ago, staring balefully at the very spot where Mr. Levy had been killed. Kelly could almost see her there now with her long gray skirt billowing around her in the breeze, much the same way that it had floated around her ankles at the beach.

"I *have* seen you before," Kelly groaned. A shudder shook her entire body, and she could feel fingers of fear gripping her spine. "Who are you? What do you want?!"

"Kelly?" Wendy's worried voice seemed to be coming from a distance. "Kelly, are you OK?"

"It's her," Kelly whispered in a trembling voice.

"Who?" Wendy looked where Kelly was staring.

"The woman in gray—she's right there!" Kelly almost screamed. But the bewildered expression on Wendy's face told Kelly her friend had no idea what she was talking about.

• • • • • • • • • • •

By Thursday Kelly had managed to stop thinking about the strange morning in the park with Wendy, and she was actually beginning to get excited about camp. Her mom and dad usually drove her to camp, but this year they had decided that, at thirteen she was old enough to ride on the train with the rest of her friends, including Maureen and Nora. Wendy's older sister and aunt were going along to be sure that everyone was OK. Besides there had been a lot of rain lately, and so there was the danger of running into a rock or mud slide up on the twisty mountain roads. Kelly's parents had decided the train would be safer.

"Are you packed yet?" Maureen asked Wendy at lunchtime.

Wendy laughed. "I've been packed all week. I don't know if can make it to Saturday. How about you, Kel?"

"I'm ready to go today," she said, smiling.

"Me, too," Nora groaned as she dropped her books on the lunch table and plopped down next to her friends.

Kelly glanced down at a newspaper clipping that had slipped from Nora's notebook. She picked it up and stared hard at the stark, black-and-white photograph.

"Where did you get this?" she demanded a little harshly.

Nora raised one eyebrow. "From the newspaper. It's for current events. A tornado in Missouri wrecked a school."

Kelly wasn't really listening. All she could see was the woman in the picture. She was standing off to the side watching, while rescue workers searched for survivors in the wreckage. It was the woman in gray.

"It's her!" Kelly nearly shouted, shoving the clipping toward Wendy and jabbing her finger at the picture of the woman. "She shows up wherever people die, and I keep seeing her!"

"What?" Nora giggled. "What are you talking about?"

Wendy laughed nervously. "She's just goofing around." She shot a serious look at Kelly. "Aren't you, Kel?"

Kelly gazed doubtfully at the clipping, and then at her friends' expressions. Finally she took a deep breath and nodded.

•••••••••••

The next day Kelly's parents drove her to the train station. Megan chattered excitedly the whole way, but Kelly barely said a word. At the station, she nervously searched the crowd, half expecting to see the dreaded woman in gray. She had seen her over and over again in her nightmares. It was always the same. The woman would appear outside the window, then draw closer and closer, staring at Kelly all the while.

"Kelly!" Wendy called out waving. "Over here!" Wendy was standing on the platform near the train with five other girls. They were all talking and laughing.

Kelly turned to her family. "I guess I'd better get going," she said with a smile, giving each of them a big hug and tickling Megan on the stomach. She picked up her backpack and walked over to join the group.

"Smile!" Maureen called out from behind her instant-picture camera. Everyone made a face just as the flash went off. Just being around her friends was already making Kelly feel a little better. In a few hours they would be in the camp van headed for two whole weeks of swimming, horseback riding, and fun. She smiled as Maureen took one shot after another.

"We'd better get aboard," Wendy's older sister said, herding the girls toward the door of the train car. Once inside, Kelly grabbed a seat by the window. She took one final, careful look at the people on the platform and let out a sigh of relief. The woman in gray wasn't among them. The train jerked slightly, then slowly began to pull out of the station.

Soon the city was left behind and the train was speeding through beautiful hill country. The other girls had rushed to the dining car for sodas, but Kelly had decided to take some time in the main car to watch the incredible scenery. From the window she could see pine forests sweeping up toward the mountaintop on one side. On the other side of the tracks, a sparkling blue river snaked through a deep ravine. It was so lovely, but she couldn't quite shake the feeling of uneasiness that still clung to her.

"What's up, Kel?" Wendy said, flopping into the seat next to her. She leaned in with a mischievous grin. "Did your mystery woman get on the train with us?"

Kelly shook her head and smiled weakly. "I know it sounds silly, but I really did see her all those times I said I did." She shrugged. "But she's not here now."

"Then stop worrying," Wendy said, smiling. She tossed the photographs that had been taken earlier into Kelly's lap. "Stop looking for someone who doesn't exist and check these out."

Kelly picked up the first one of the whole group making faces at the camera, and she laughed out loud. She held up the next photograph and the smile faded from her lips. There, seated on the train and gazing out the window directly at the girls, was the woman in gray. Kelly could barely breathe.

"She's here!" she gasped in horror. "Look, she's been here all along and I didn't . . . "

All at once Kelly heard the squeal of metal on metal and she was thrown forward. The train lurched heavily to one side as it struck the slide of boulders that had fallen across the tracks only minutes before.

"What's happening!?" Wendy shrieked as she clung to her seat. Then she was tossed like a rag doll into the aisle and knocked out cold.

Kelly managed to push herself back into her own seat. Terror gripped every nerve of her body as she saw the woman in gray standing at the car entrance.

"NO!!" Kelly cried out. "Stay away from me!" But the woman moved slowly toward her, oblivious to the screams of the other passengers.

"It's your turn now," the woman whispered, reaching out her pale hand. Filled with dread, Kelly realized that the woman's eyes were no longer hidden. For the first time she was able to stare directly into their sorrowful depths . . . and her fear drained away. Reaching out her own hand, Kelly lightly touched the woman's long, cold fingers and felt a sense of calm.

"It's time to go," the woman said softly. Kelly rose, pausing only for a moment to glance at her own lifeless body sprawled in the aisle, a terrible wound across her forehead. "Don't worry," the woman added. "There will be many others going with us."

With a sickening groan the train tumbled from the tracks like a huge beast, then rolled down the steep embankment and into the ravine below.

———>•◇•<———

Horror in the Center Ring

aul slammed his locker door, and Martin raised his eyebrows looking at his friend. "What's bothering you?" he asked.

"My mom said I can't go to the pool party at Tara's house on Saturday because my room's a mess," Paul said in disgust. "I have to spend Saturday cleaning it."

"That's the pits," Martin said sympathetically. "It's *your* room. You should be able to keep it any way you want. My dad is always on my case too: Do *this*. Do *that*."

"All parents ever do is nag," Paul grumbled. "It seems like I never do anything right. I ought to just leave home. Then I could do whatever I want."

"Yeah," Martin agreed. "That would be great, but where could we go? We'd have to get jobs or something."

Paul studied the floor thoughtfully. "I don't know . . . yet. But I'll think of something. I'd do anything to be out on my own."

• • • • • • • • • • •

Over the next two weeks, Paul and Martin talked of nothing but what they would do if they left home.

"Look," Martin said excitedly as they walked to school one morning, pulling a folded bright yellow flyer from his pocket and waving it in the air.

Paul grabbed the paper, opened it, and read the heading aloud: "OLD WORLD CIRCUS . . . SEE EXOTIC ANIMALS FROM ALL OVER THE GLOBE . . . THRILL TO DEATH DEFYING ACTS." He turned and looked quizzically at Martin. "Sounds OK, but so what?"

"Think about it," Martin answered, tapping the side of his head with his finger. "Last year I read a book about a kid who ran away and joined the circus. It's perfect. No school. And it's like an unwritten rule or something in the circus that nobody asks any questions."

Paul glanced down and saw that the opening day parade was scheduled for that weekend.

"They'll be in town for three days," Martin continued. "And I say that when they leave, we go with them."

"Oh, come on," Paul said skeptically. "They're not going to take us. They could get in trouble."

"Not if we hide out in one of their vans," Martin assured him. "We could sneak in at night. By the time they find us, we'll be a zillion miles from this crummy place. Maybe I can even learn to be a lion tamer! I'd love to be in an act like that with the big cats."

Paul reread the flyer. "Well," he said, nodding, "at least we can check it out."

And so on Saturday morning, Paul and Martin rode their bikes to Main Street early. They found a good spot close to the curb and waited with expectation for the circus parade the flyer had mentioned. Before long, dozens of other happy spectators joined them, and soon afterward the merry sound of approaching calliope music blended with the buzz of the crowd.

"Look! Look, an elephant!" a little girl squealed delightedly. Paul craned his neck to see the huge animal rounding the corner at the end of the block. The enormous creature was wearing a colorful cape with spangles that glittered in the sun. On its head was a cap topped with tall, fluffy feathers. Behind the elephant was a parade of masked performers, clowns, and several costumed people on tall stilts.

"Wow," Martin exclaimed as the lion and tiger cages approached. "Look at that!" The impressive cats roared threateningly at the crowd. The beasts paced back and forth, seemingly upset and anxious. Riding atop one of the cages was a man dressed in a black silk tuxedo. He had a top hat and a long, dark cape lined with crimson silk the color of blood. In his hand he held a whip, which he cracked every now and then.

Paul stared in awe at the man, who as he passed in front of the boys turned and gave them a knowing grin.

"He must be the ringmaster," Martin commented.

"This is the coolest thing I've ever seen," Paul exclaimed, watching as the elephant led the parade on its way to the fairgrounds. "I'd do anything to be a part of the circus. Do you really think we could just . . . "

All at once a shadow fell across the two boys, and Paul became silent. He turned to see a tall clown leaning over him and Martin. In spite of his painted-on smile, the clown seemed more menacing than funny. He held out a silvery helium balloon to Paul.

"Is that for me?" Paul asked apprehensively.

The clown didn't answer. He simply smiled wider, exposing a row of sparkling white teeth. Slowly Paul reached up to take the balloon.

"Whoa!" he blurted out, jerking his hand back and letting go of the string. The icy cold touch of the clown's long fingers had taken him by surprise. Looking up, he watched as the balloon escaped, floating higher and higher into the air. The clown backed away and took his place in the parade.

"What was that about?" Martin asked.

"I'm not sure," Paul answered, trying to rub the clown's chill from his fingers.

• • • • • • • • • • •

That night Paul was awakened by the sound of his mother's worried voice on the telephone. He listened carefully but only caught snatches of conversation.

"How long?" he heard his mom ask. "No, I haven't . . . he's asleep . . . I'll ask him. . . . Don't worry, I'm sure he won't go far. . . . You can't blame yourself. . . . I'll call you back."

Paul shut his eyes and pretended to be asleep as his mom opened his bedroom door. "Paul?" she said gently.

He didn't move.

"Paul?" she said a little louder. "Please wake up. It's about Martin."

Paul opened his eyes and asked, "What about Martin?"

His mother seemed worried. "I just spoke to his dad. It seems that they had a big fight tonight, and now Martin is missing. His backpack is gone, too. Do you have any idea where he might be? Has he said anything to you about running away?"

"No," Paul lied. He tried hard to keep his voice as steady as possible. "I don't know anything."

"Are you sure?" his mom asked again. "This is really important. His parents are frantic."

"I said I didn't know," Paul mumbled, rolling over and pretending to go back to sleep. As soon as his mom left his room, he jumped up and pulled on jeans, a sweatshirt, and a pair of sneakers. He had already prepared his backpack with snacks, bottled water, and some extra clothes.

"This wasn't the plan," he grumbled to himself as he slipped out of his bedroom window and headed for the fairgrounds. "What is Martin doing? He's gonna mess up everything."

• • • • • • • • • • •

The circus grounds seemed eerily quiet. Paul slipped into the main tent and looked around. "Martin," he called out in a harsh whisper, but his voice echoed off the empty stands.

"How am I supposed to find him now?" Paul muttered, backing toward the exit. Then all at once he felt himself gripped powerfully at the shoulders.

"I thought you might be along soon to join your friend." Paul twisted around to look into the shadowy face of the ringmaster from the parade.

"Is Martin here?" Paul asked in a shaky voice.

"Indeed," the man said, releasing his hold. "We always welcome runaways. In fact," he added in a sinister tone, "they are a very important part of this *particular* circus." The ringmaster leaned in toward Paul. "So what is it, my boy? Parents don't understand you? A problem with school? No matter . . . we have a place for you here. I think you will fit in quite well."

Paul noticed movement behind the ringmaster and saw that three other performers had entered the tent. The odd clown from the parade was among them.

"I—I've changed my mind," he said fearfully. "I want to go home."

"I'm afraid it's too late for that." The ringmaster laughed coldly, then reached out for him.

"No!" Paul shouted, dodging to the side of the ringmaster. Managing to evade the scowling clown and the others, he raced from the tent.

But when he got to the exit, he saw that it was now blocked by several creepy-looking circus performers. He quickly pressed himself into the shadows along the tent, almost tasting the fear that was welling up inside of him. Then looking from left to right, he made a dash to the shelter of the fun house wall. He took cover behind a large decorative cage parked beside the wall. Nearby, the low rumble of a lion gave him chills. His only thought was of getting away from this terrible place and back to the safety of his own home. Once he was there he would never complain about anything again, and he'd keep his room sparkling clean.

All at once Paul heard his name being called softly. It was his friend's voice, but it sounded strangely different . . . altered . . . as if Martin were having trouble forming the words. "Martin, where are you?" Paul demanded.

"Here!" the deep, foreign-sounding voice responded from the cage behind him.

Paul turned cautiously. And then he felt as if the world had suddenly flipped upside down. There in front of him was his best friend . . . changed . . . transformed into some sort of horrifying mutant—half tiger, half human.

"Martin?" Paul croaked, barely able to recognize his friend.

Where Martin had once had hands and feet, he now had large paws tipped with gleaming black talons. His face was covered with coarse orange and black fur, and his extended snout ended in a mouth filled with sharp, ivory-colored fangs. "You've got to get away while you still can and get help. It's our only hope," Martin moaned. "The ringmaster has some sort of power. He'll do it to you, too," he warned, holding out his large paws.

"The ringmaster?" Paul asked, staring at his friend with a mixture of fascination and horror. "But how did he do this to you?"

"I don't know for sure," Martin said. "But whatever you do, don't put on—" He stopped abruptly and shrank back in

fear. "They're coming!" Martin shrieked, retreating to the back of his cage. "Hide!"

Without hesitation, Paul darted through the curtained entrance to the fun house. It was dully lit inside by tiny bulbs along the floor that led the way through the gloomy corridor.

Slowly, carefully, Paul edged along, straining to hear if anyone was coming after him. Then turning a corner, he suddenly came face to face with dozens of mirror images of himself, all grotesque and distorted. Choking back a scream, he put out his hands and pressed his fingers against the glass, trying to feel for an exit out of the horrible place.

Dripping with sweat caused by fear and the hot, stagnant air surrounding him, Paul felt as if he would suffocate if he didn't escape soon. All around him were deformed apparitions of himself trapped in the mirrors reflecting his panic, which grew as he heard the sounds of someone entering the fun house and moving deliberately toward him.

Hurrying along, Paul suddenly stumbled through an unmirrored archway and into a small room that appeared to be used for storage. He looked around for a good hiding place, but saw only disorderly piles of clothing, masks, and props. In desperation, he burrowed under a mound of silky costumes, but found that there wasn't quite enough to cover him . . . and the sound of footsteps was getting closer.

What am I going to do? his mind raced, near hysteria. Then he noticed an elaborate mask. With only seconds to spare, he slipped it over his head so that he was completely concealed. Holding his breath, he remained perfectly still as someone stepped into the room, apparently looked around, and then left.

Breathing a sigh of relief, Paul slid from his hiding place and tried to pull the confining mask from his head. But it wouldn't budge. Clawing at it in growing terror, he stumbled back into the hall of mirrors. From dozens of different angles, he saw himself with the ferocious head of a tiger.

"No!" he screamed, running through the dark corridor as the mask burned into his own skin.

Once outside, Paul found himself surrounded by a dozen glaring performers. "Get it off me!" he screamed to them. "Please, get it off!" But the words were difficult for Paul to form with the long, sharp teeth that were emerging from his growing snout, and they came out sounding deep and foreign.

The ringmaster stepped forward and grabbed him by the arm. "Your new home is ready," the man announced with a sneer. He twisted Paul around to look at the cage that had once held his best friend. Now a wild tiger paced back and forth inside.

"You and your friend wanted to join the circus," the ringmaster snarled. "Well, you got your wish." He shoved Paul roughly into the cage with what was once Martin. "Now you boys play nicely!" He laughed cruelly. "You're going to be together for a very long time."